SLAUGHTERHOUSE BLUES

More titles by Nick Kolakowski

(Shotgun Honey Books)

A Brutal Bunch of Heartbroken Saps
Main Bad Guy
Hell of a Mess
Love & Bullets: Megabomb Edition
Payback is Forever

(Down & Out Books)

Boise Long Pig Club
Rattlesnake Rodeo
Maxine Unleashes Doomsday

(Other releases)

Absolute Unit
Lockdown:
Stories of Crime, Terror, and Hope During a Pandemic

A LOVE & BULLETS HOOKUP
BOOK TWO

SLAUGHTER HOUSE BLUES

NICK KOLAKOWSKI

2022

SLAUGHTERHOUSE BLUES
Text copyright © 2018, 2019, 2022 Nick Kolakowski

Published by Shotgun Honey Books

215 Loma Road
Charleston, WV 25314
www.ShotgunHoney.com

Cover by Bad Fido.

ISBN-10: 1-956957-18-9
ISBN-13: 978-1-956957-64-8

9 8 7 6 5 4 3 2   22 21 20 19 18 17

To G, M, and C.

SLAUGHERHOUSE BLUES

PART ONE

GOOD DEATHS ALL AROUND

1

JAMES DYZEK PUSHED a thin blade through the Wehrmacht lieutenant's eye-socket until the brainpan cracked and the man trembled and went still. Everybody knew the war was ending and that anyone taken prisoner today would walk away free in a month or two and so James took the time to kill every Nazi he met. He had watched too many friends die to leave any of the enemy alive in good conscience.

Four decades later James would read a history book that described Americans in those last days of the European War as tired of killing. No such folks existed in his platoon. They bayoneted every Nazi they saw, raided every house they passed, pocketed every coin or trinket they could find. Once he tied a screaming German lady to the hood of his jeep, thinking it would make even a

Nazi hesitate before taking a shot, only to change his mind after a sniper pumped two bullets into her spine. He carried a pearl-handled pistol like his idol George S. Patton but preferred the knife for close work. Years later he would use the same blade to cut meat at the neighborhood barbeques he hosted at his home in Queens and nothing about that fact struck him as odd or sacrilegious.

James pulled the blade from the German's eye-socket and wiped the brains on the grass. He shook some of the splatter off his boots. That evening he soaped his pits and crotch and submitted to the icy field shower, the blood on his skin mixing with the mud. After showering, he made sure the small bag retrieved from the lieutenant's pocket was safely tucked away in his pack.

In his old age James would view the War as the finest time of his life.

Later he would challenge his sons to push-up contests, laughing every time the kids collapsed while he pumped on and on and on. Later he would leave his respectable house in the middle of the night and drive to the unrespectable parts of town and throw a burning bottle through a random window and speed away as the flames licked the black sky. Later he would inherit his father's bar and preside over endless nights of wild debauchery.

2

JAMES'S FATHER OPENED the bar near Union Square in 1938, and spent forty years collecting coins and crumpled dollars from half of New York City in exchange for glasses of foamy beer and whiskey shots. James's father kept an oversized American flag pinned to the wall beside the front door, and liked to proclaim to anyone who would listen—and they all listened, thinking he might pour them a free drink—that his bar functioned as the world's last true democracy: that anyone, whether a greengrocer or a tailor from the Garment District or a Wall Street trader, could slap down a quarter for a boilermaker and take a seat on one of the chipped stools and voice an opinion.

When James came back from Europe he would spend his afternoons sitting beneath the flag, listening to the dried-out old men talk about horrors they witnessed in the First World War. He understood that they wanted to relate to him. In those years James worked for a butcher off Cooper Square and walked around the neighborhood in his bloody apron, and when he sat beneath the flag it was usually with a couple handfuls of peanuts, which he would shell and eat while nodding at those recollections of Belleau Wood and Blanc Mont Ridge and Hamel and the Second Battle of the Marne, mud and gangrene and artillery.

Before he met his wife and moved to Queens, James would use the bar's dingy closet of a bathroom to shave in the mornings, and oftentimes sleep atop the bar. He wanted to stay close to the valuables he had brought back from Germany, which he kept in a locked steel box on the bottom shelf of his father's safe in the back room. When his father started asking too many questions about the box, James hid it beneath the floorboards.

3

AFTER HIS FATHER lost his mind, James had to shave him twice a week. His father's skin had gone slack with age and James needed to pinch him beneath the jaw in order to smooth his cheeks enough for the razor. His father's pupils staring into him the whole time, deep and merciless as black holes. Although his father could still dress himself, sometimes James would come over to the house and find the old man sitting in his own piss, his thighs red and raw.

The woman paid to watch his father was good at preventing him from leaving the stove on, or tumbling down the stairs, or torturing the cat, but sometimes he fought when she tried to change him, and she would call James, who always spent the drive to his father's house yelling about how much time and money this all cost him, this refusal to die. Yet every time he came through the door with his fists balled and his face twisted in anger, his father adopted a look of such childlike contrition that it sent guilt slamming like a nail through James's guts, and he wasted hours doing the laundry, the dishes, and all the other chores his father would never notice.

That guilt never lasted. His father wandered around the house looking for his long-dead brother, or pissed into bottles that he left in the fridge. His father placed the radio in the stove and turned on the heat. On those bad days James would contemplate his famous knife, and whether the time had come for a long drive, just the two of them, into the forests upstate. James had killed a couple dozen men in Europe but ending your father's life is something else, even if your father has a head of broken clockwork.

One winter afternoon, on the woman's day off, James came over with groceries and found his father stiff and dead on the couch, and that was okay, it was better than shipping the old man off to a hospital to wind down his last months under the bored watch of nurses. James put the paper sacks on the table and sat on the couch and held his father's cold hand, rubbing his thumb over skin translucent as parchment. Outside the snow dissolved the world in white.

4

AFTER HIS FATHER died, James refused to change much about the bar, besides replacing the long maple stick beneath the register with a baseball bat. Every morning he opened the rear door to the dogs skulking in the alley and fed them organ meat donated by his old friends in the butcher business. When a health inspector tried to lecture him about the presence of canines in an establishment serving food and drink, James made a great show of taking the baseball bat from behind the bar and thwacking its barrel into his palm until the man left.

James quit drinking the day he inherited the bar, preferring to nurse a soda water while the men around him downed gallons of beer and harder stuff. To anyone who asked, James said he had no intention of slurping away his margins. He let undercover cops rub shoulders with the butchers and salesmen and artists, because he believed in law and order and the city around them roughened by the day. His sons were cowards and so he made them run drinks and break up fights in order to toughen them up for a hard world.

No matter how often people suggested he update the furniture, or at least vacuum the floor, James left the interior untouched. Portraits of John Brown and Theodore Roosevelt glowered from ornate frames above the liquor shelves, and the rococo mirror beside the bathroom door miraculously survived every brawl. Before he opened the bar to the day's drinkers, James would always head into the back room and unscrew the three floorboards nearest the north wall and peek into the space beneath, where that battered metal box contained his riches from overseas.

His retirement, as he thought of it.

His *treasure*.

PART TWO

BORN TO RUN

1

KEEP JABBERING ABOUT the Dusty Brothers Memorial Stripper Pole, Fiona muttered under her breath, and I swear I'll paint the walls of this bar with your guts.

The man across the table from her, John Dusty, raised his sun-reddened hands to mime how the local strip club's only pole had torn free of its bolts after too many years of vigorous use. His thick fingers flicked the air as he described how much "humanitarian aid" he delivered the next morning, in the form of a shopping bag stuffed with American dollars. That generous assistance helped put the hard-working employees of the Pussy Cat Disco back on their glittery five-inch heels within two days. "I even had the manufacturer make a little plaque for the new pole," he laughed. "It reads: 'In gratitude of all you've done, love, John and Don Dusty.'"

Fiona's hand drifted beneath the hem of her loose linen shirt, skimming the checkered grip of the automatic strapped to her hip. John was a mountainous dude, his frayed black tank-top barely holding back an avalanche of flesh, but a bullet has a nice way of reducing everyone to the same level.

A half-second on the draw and pull, she mused. Then, peace and quiet, once the bystanders stopped screaming.

So quick, so easy.

But ending her jackass client's existence would have meant dealing with the local cops, not to mention returning to Managua without a payday. Chewing the inside of her cheek, Fiona settled back in her seat and wondered when the waitress would deliver their food. Beside her, John's reed-thin brother Don sipped his lukewarm beer and stared at her chest with an intensity that suggested he was trying to gauge her cup size.

God, she hated these two.

Good thing they always paid in cash, half in advance.

John plowed onward: "In fact, this one little señorita, she's so overcome with happiness that she shows up at the factory a couple days later, offering to give me a lap dance right there in the office, and I…"

"I got a question," Fiona interrupted.

"Can I finish?" John frowned.

"In a sec," she said. "Before your ego gets too inflated and you float right off the face of the earth, I want to talk business. It was a long drive up. Why am I here?"

John fired an artillery round of a glare at Don, who shuddered in response. "Bro, she's right," Don said. "It's getting late."

"Late for you, maybe." Slugging down the last of his beer, John slammed down the glass hard enough to startle the nearby barflies. "Not for me, though. Since we gifted the pole, the club's always open."

The waitress arrived, bearing two steaming platters of grilled goat mixed with vegetables and rice. The bartender on her heels held three full pints of beer to his chest. The glorious smell of food roasting in well-seasoned iron made Fiona's stomach rumble. The one silver lining of driving through the Nicaraguan highlands to Estelí was the opportunity to eat at El Porrón, a bar that, like the neighborhood around it, offered some treasures behind its rough exterior.

Without waiting for either brother to make a move, Fiona popped a sizzling-hot shred of goat in her mouth, washing it down with a mouthful of beer. "Business," she said. "It was a rough trip, and I want to get some shut-eye."

Don scanned the establishment for anyone within earshot. The three scruffy amigos on the far side of the bar cared more about their respective glasses than a conversation at the corner table. "We're being blackmailed," he said. "They want money we don't have, or they'll burn the factory down."

"The factory's concrete," Fiona said. "You got guards, fences."

John snorted and shook his head. "Someone torches the tobacco we got curing, the storerooms, we're out a couple years of stock. And sure, we could hire even more guards, but who knows if that'll work? Maybe it's an inside job."

"Other firms hear about our troubles, they'll make a

play for our most skilled rollers, our back-office guys," Don added. "There are eight big cigar companies in town, including us. Competition's too tight for any disruption, you get me?"

"Loud and clear," Fiona said. "Any idea who's doing the blackmailing?"

"We got suspects." John shoveled down goat.

"All seven rivals," Don laughed.

"You're not paying me enough to start a war." Fiona slid a hand to her hip, drawing their eyes to the outline of her pistol. "I'm here to mop up a problem, spritz with cleanser, leave everything all shiny. That means you give me real leads, okay? What you got?"

Don frowned and crossed his arms. "Last night, someone throws a Molotov cocktail over the fence, hits that mural we had painted last summer. You know the one I'm talking about?"

Fiona sighed. A decade ago, these brothers, in the throes of a shared midlife crisis, started their foray into cigar-making with money from their small liquor-distribution business. They had built their factory a kilometer outside of Estelí, and filled it with two hundred employees who spent six days a week rolling dark Nicaraguan and Honduran tobacco leaves into cancer-sticks that sold for two hundred dollars a box. It was a sweet living, and a nice success story, but Fiona always winced when she took the curve near their property and saw a three-story-tall swimsuit model looming above the trees, a porno leer on her face as she brandished a pair of pink Uzis.

The brothers could afford to grow up a little.

Good thing they always paid in cash, half in advance.

"She's seen it," John said, reading her face. "Anyway, mural's wrecked, but we figured it's just someone wilding out. Until early this morning, when this kid shows up on a motorbike at the gate."

"You know the kid?" Fiona asked.

John shook his head. "Kept his helmet on the whole time, guard said. Visor down. Kid says get together five hundred thousand cash, that's U.S. dollars, be ready to deliver it by tomorrow at noon, or the whole place goes up in flames."

"Guard try to stop him?"

"Sure. And when he did, the kid pulled out some dinky pistol, shot him in the leg, drove off. Our nurse pulled out the bullet, guard's fine. We called you right after. We're taking this as a serious threat."

"You call the cops?"

Don shook his head. "You know the cops won't do crap."

That was good. The fewer *Policía Nacional* involved here, the better. "Where's the drop-off?"

"They haven't given us details. Said get the money together, wait for the call." John downed his pint in a single gulp, wiped the foam from his lips, and snapped his fingers at the bartender. "Whoever it is, we're not paying. We just don't have the liquidity. So we need you to grab whoever shows up, follow the trail from there."

"You know the deal: three thousand a day," Fiona said. "Minimum five days, plus expenses."

"Oh, come on." Don rolled his eyes. "How much money have we given you over the past couple months? We deserve a friends and family discount, or something."

"You're not friends, and you're not family. That's my rate." She scooped up a fresh load of animal protein and chewed it slowly, letting the silence build.

From his hip pocket, John pulled out one of his signature cigars, tore off the tip with his teeth, and spat a glistening nub of tobacco on the floor. Don slipped a butane lighter from his pocket and torched his brother's smoke.

"Fine," John said, exhaling a long white plume. "Fifteen grand to save half a million, not so bad, right?"

"It's good math," Fiona agreed, wrinkling her nose at the stench of burning tobacco. "And I get half up front, as always."

Another long pause from the brothers, mostly for theater's sake, before Don reached into the bag at his feet and slapped a padded envelope the size of a brick on the table. Fiona nodded her thanks and slipped it into her own bag.

"Where you staying?" John asked. "Need a room anywhere?"

"I'm right around the corner," Fiona said. That was a lie. A healthy sense of paranoia had kept her upright and breathing far longer than anyone expected, especially herself. "Don't worry about me, guys."

"So as I was saying about this little señorita..." John shifting gears again, as the waiter brought him a fresh pint.

Fiona tuned him out, vaguely hoping his beer contained a generous load of spit, courtesy of the bartender. Her seat offered a view of the bar's front door, open to the night. She heard the mosquito whine of an approaching car, a click, and an amplified voice hollering in Spanish: one of the propaganda vehicles that circled these neighborhoods at all hours, pumping out slogans at ear-bursting volume. Headlights brightened the crumbling curb beyond the door, driving away a bony dog.

"By the way, at this point I can recognize half these chicks just by their tattoos…'"

As it passed the bar, the car backfired, loud as a shotgun blast. John yipped and dove for the floor, hitting hard enough to rattle every plate and chair in the room. His flailing arm smacked the legs of Don's chair, and then both brothers were down, roaring in surprise and pain.

Fiona bit a knuckle to stop her laughter. "Nervous much, boys?" she asked sweetly.

Don't humiliate them, murmured the saner voice in her head. You need the money. Without it, you and Bill are dead.

2

BILL KNEW THE bastards were following him.

Maybe he should have dressed a little less conspicuously, but the white seersucker suit had called to him as he rifled through his luggage that morning. Paired with a straw hat, a cornflower-blue dress shirt, and a natty bow-tie, he looked every inch the Hemingway character as he exited the five-star Meliá Cohíba, a block away from the crumbling splendor of the Malecón, the road that separates Havana from the sea. Weeks of dressing like a stereotypical tourist, in T-shirts and baggy shorts, had sickened his soul.

He hungered for a decent meal, a difficult thing to find in the state-run hotels, where the employees swiped the best stuff behind the scenes. Those stolen morsels often found their way to the *paladars*, or the small restaurants that Cubans ran out of their homes. A concierge had recommended a good one a half-kilometer from the Cohíba, claiming the family there served the best coffee in Havana, provided you were copacetic with drinking it beside a coop that housed an irate rooster.

Crossing the Malecón to the crumbling sea-wall, he paused to reach into his jacket and extract a flat alligator-skin case. Inside sat a trio of Dusty Brothers cigars. Yesterday morning Fiona had left for their factory in Nicaragua, to solve some sort of problem. Bill had never met the guys himself, but he knew they paid her a lot of money to do their dirty work, and always sent her home with a fresh box of smokes. Cupping a lit match in his hands, he torched the smallest of the cigars. The smell and the smoke he could take or leave, but the nicotine really helped him think.

Truth be told, he needed a few days away from his girlfriend. If you think relationships are hard, try maintaining one while on the run from some of the worst people alive. Sure, Bill drank when stressed out, and sometimes let his mouth run a little—that didn't give Fiona the right to throw things at his head, or tell him over and over again to get his crap together.

He missed the days when they would lie in bed until eleven, find something sugary to eat, and spend the afternoon listening to music while Fiona cleaned her guns. Nothing big or fancy: just living life. During the worst night of their escape, chained in a redneck psycho's basement, Bill had clung to those memories the way someone religious might grip a crucifix. But even in Havana, their old routine failed to return; they were too wired, counting and recounting their cash, jumpy at the sound of footfalls and loud voices.

Returning the case to his pocket, Bill noticed the man and woman standing fifty yards further down the Malecón. They were dressed like the vacationing Europeans who filled this section of the city: linen shirts, khaki pants for him and a knee-length red skirt for her, their faces hidden by sunglasses and wide-brim straw hats.

Something about the couple set Bill's inner alarm wailing. Maybe it was how they kept glancing his way. Or how their hands stayed in their pockets.

Bill breathed smoke and strode with purpose in the opposite direction. At this hour of morning, swarms of kids dashed along the low wall to his left, breaking around the old men sunning themselves on the concrete. A few stopped their frantic activity long enough to ask Bill for a peso; he waved them off. Another quick look over his shoulder confirmed the worst: the couple was following him, fast. From twenty yards away, he could see the man was hulking as a football player, the woman small and lithe.

What did they want?

When you make a living by ripping folks off, the list of those who want you dead becomes very, very long after a few decades.

Top of the Kill Bill list: the crew in the Dominican Republic who had offered Bill protection after he ran out on his old employers, the Rockaway Mob. After a few weeks, Bill and Fiona had decided the "security" came at too high a price, and took their leave. Maybe he shouldn't have left with a big chunk of the crew's money.

Competing for the number-one spot on that same list: the Rockaway Mob. A group of scary dudes back in New York City who wrecked things better than a herd of bulls in an antique shop. It was fun when the bulls were on your side, and you wanted that antique shop stomped flat, but it was far less entertaining when those horns thirsted for your blood. Maybe he shouldn't have left with a big chunk of their money, either.

And if you excluded those two fine groups, you still had thirty-odd years of rubes itching for a shot at Bill's head. Hell, for all he knew, his fifth-grade teacher had signed away part of her retirement savings to a hit team as retribution for Bill stealing her car back in the day.

"I should've been an accountant," Bill sighed.

It was suicidal to stay in the open. He waited for a break in traffic and trotted across the Malecón again at Calle 19, skirting the elegant hulk of the Hotel Nacional. On the opposite curb he stopped and turned, cigar clenched between his lips, waiting to see what the couple did next. He was reasonably certain neither one carried a pistol. When you arrived at José Martí Airport, just outside of Havana, the customs agents ran your bags and bodies through metal detectors. The regime's paranoia made it almost impossible to buy a gun on the street.

But knives were pretty easy to find.

The couple stopped across from Bill as the Malecón swelled anew with Russian-made taxis and ancient Fords. Their sunglasses and hats mostly hid their features, aside from sharp jawlines. The woman had slashed her mouth with a deep red lipstick that made it look like a wound.

Just as quickly as it appeared, the traffic began to slacken again. A beautiful battleship of a '57 Chevy, all fins and polished chrome, slid to a stop in front of Bill. The young driver craned his head toward the open passenger window, asking if señor needed a ride somewhere for cheap.

Yes, señor most definitely needed a ride, price no object.

Opening the heavy rear door, Bill slid into the backseat. "*Vamos!*" The Chevy heaved onto the road, its joints creaking as it picked up speed. Bill stuck his hand out the window and offered the disappearing couple a proud middle finger.

The driver asked him slowly: *¿"Adónde quieres ir?"*

Bill settled into his seat, puffing his cigar. His nerves demanded something a little stronger than *paladar* coffee. In halting Spanish, he told the man to take him to El Florid-ita, one of the most notable drinking-holes in town, where the bartenders could whip him up one or three world-class daiquiris. As the Chevy squeezed through avenues clogged with antique cruisers, the fear struck Bill hard as a bullet:

Of course they hadn't chased him. Morning on the Malecón meant too many witnesses and cops, in a country that doubled as a jail.

They were testing his perimeter, seeing how he reacted.

And they knew where he was staying.

3

FIONA SPENT THE night in her usual Estelí haunt, a small apartment above a coffin store in Barrio Villa Esperanza, on the city's eastern edge. The luxurious accommodations included a bare mattress on a low wooden platform, a small desk teetering on a splintered leg, and a window that opened onto the next-door neighbor's roof. She paid the coffin store's owner fifty bucks a night to stay up there, and in return for that princely sum he asked no questions. He also allowed her to park her rental jeep a few blocks away, in a garage he owned.

"One change from last time," the owner told her in Spanish, after unlocking the apartment door and ushering her inside. "Do not use the shower."

"Why?" Fiona peeked into the tiled shower stall. "Does it bite?"

"Heater's broken. The wires, it's a mess."

As with more than a few bathrooms in this part of the world, the shower-head included a built-in heating element. Cold water from the pipes flowed over a hot, insulated coil inside the unit before jetting out the nozzle at a piss-warm temperature. Stepping into the stall, Fiona saw a deep crack in the shower-head's plastic shell. If that wasn't worrisome enough, the electrical cord that snaked from the back of the unit to a hole in the ceiling looked a little frayed.

"Zap," Fiona said.

The man nodded. "Zap."

"Guess I'm not cleaning up."

Once she settled in, she powered up her phone and tried Bill. Eight rings before it cut to voicemail. A minute later she tried again. Still no answer. She tried to squelch the fright prickling her belly. He's probably asleep, she told herself. Passed out drunk, like he did every time she left.

Or maybe he's not picking up because he's still mad at you, a nasty little demon whispered. You keep saying he's too soft for this fugitive thing, but maybe you're too hard, too quick with the gun. You shot that man in Oklahoma when he tried to help you—

He was a killer. Shut up.

Or maybe Bill's dead. Maybe someone finally came up behind him on the street and put a bullet in his skull, or a knife between his ribs, and you weren't there to save him—

"Shut up," she whispered to the empty room.

After sending Bill a text, she forced herself to go to

sleep. If she had to worry, she preferred to do so on a full night's rest.

The owner had provided two thin pillows and a stack of blankets. After piling most of the bedding into a roughly human-shaped form on the bed, she retired to the bathroom, where she spread one of the blankets on the floor of the shower stall and curled up there, her pistol and phone in easy reach. Without air conditioning, the night was humid and still. Sweat trickled from her skin as she slept fitfully, dreaming of dead Bill afloat in the middle of the ocean, the jacket of his fabulous suit billowing in the current.

When she woke up, her phone displayed no new voice-mails or texts. Her worry sprouted claws and fangs, ripped at her insides. She did a hundred push-ups to exhaust it, dressed in a T-shirt and jeans, and headed outside for a cup of coffee.

Following a hefty dose of caffeine, along with a jumbo bottle of water to replenish her sweat reservoir, Fiona drove across town to meet with one of her old contacts, easing the jeep through narrow streets teeming with kids kicking soccer balls, whining dirt-bikes, factory workers stuffed in rattletrap sedans, dogs nosing through rubble in search of scraps. The bright stucco walls still scarred from a civil war decades in the past. She took a left down a dirt alley, followed by a hard right into an open garage, parking beside a rusty pickup missing its wheels.

Shutting off the engine, Fiona climbed out of the jeep and unlocked the rear hatch. A door opened in the back of the garage, framing an old man in khakis and a starched white shirt: Ortiz. She noted his bare feet, the skin toughened to callus, three toes missing thanks to a Sandinista torture session.

After giving her a fierce hug, Ortiz reached into the bed of the pickup and whipped back an oily tarp, unveiling a very special payload.

"Will this do?" he asked, smiling because he already knew her answer.

"Yes, it most certainly will," she replied, reaching into her back pocket for a fat wad of American dollars.

"How is your father?"

"He's good," she said, handing over the cash. "Enjoying retirement, smoking too damn much. He sends his love."

"When you speak to him again, please tell him that Luis still enjoys the chickens. He will understand." Ortiz chuckled softly.

"Sure thing." *I don't even want to know what that's in reference to,* she thought. *Two old wolves making in-jokes about the bad old days in Black Ops, when her Dear Old Dad helped plant more than a few bodies in the hills around here.*

On the return trip to the apartment she tried Bill twice. No answer. She was tempted to drop everything and drive back to Managua, catch the first flight to Havana. But the Dusty brothers had paid her half in advance, and that meant seeing the job through.

In her apartment again, after changing into a loose linen shirt, she armed herself. A handful of plastic riot-cuffs went in the left back pocket of her jeans, along with an extra pistol magazine in her right. She checked the spring release on the push dagger nested in her oversized belt buckle. With those tasks complete, she stripped down and rebuilt her pistol—a regular habit before every mission, and one that served her well.

Before leaving, Fiona undertook one final task. Sure, she could have rented a room practically anywhere in town, but this one offered another advantage over a hotel. The push dagger slipped neatly into a crack between the floorboards in one corner of the main room. A little tug, and a trapdoor sprung open on a hinge, exposing a crawl-space. Another artifact of the civil war. She slipped her bag into the hole and lowered the hinge again.

Separating from the money gave her a jolt of anxiety, but the hidey-hole was the safest place for it until she returned. Back in the jeep, she phoned Bill. Still nothing. She needed to finish this job as fast as possible and leave.

It was a pleasant drive out to the Dusty Brothers' cigar factory, a low red building on a hill overlooking the muddy churn of the Rio Estelí. On the approach, the bikini mural flickered into view through the trees, its bottom half scorched to ash, the model's smile blackened. The two guards at the gate waved her through without a word, and she parked beyond the glittering rows of work-ers' bicycles.

Don appeared in a doorway, dressed in a T-shirt with the Captain America shield on it, puffing on a stubby cigar. "You're a little early," he said, barely meeting her eyes. Probably embarrassed after last night. Nobody likes falling on their ass in a public place.

"I like to shake things up," she said, noting how his hands quaked.

"Want some coffee? We got time to kill."

"Sure."

The interior of the factory was raw industrial space. Don escorted her through the rolling room, sunlit by tall windows covered with steel mesh. At rows of wooden desks, rollers smoothed out tobacco leaves on thick boards before trimming the edges with their curved *chaveta* blades. The clacking of steel blended into a backbeat to the Latin pop pounding from the speakers bolted to the walls.

Fiona watched a nearby worker expertly stuff a tight handful of filler leaves into a wooden mold. The wrapper leaf went over that molded bundle, followed by a small cap held in place with vegetable paste. Floor inspectors walked between the rows, examining finished cigars in the wooden bins atop the desks. Fiona knew from previous visits that the cigars would end up in boxes in the *escaparates*, cool chambers deep inside the factory, where they would age for months. That is, unless someone lit the place on fire.

They climbed a flight of concrete stairs to the lounge. A pair of coffee-makers hummed on a table at the far end, beside a pair of plush leather couches that had seen better days. Along the longest wall gleamed a spray-painted canvas, cartoon soldiers firing bolts of light at a purple tentacled monster. Large windows overlooked the rolling room.

"Where's John?" Fiona asked, as Don plucked two empty cups from the stack beside the machines and went to work.

"Out," Don said. "He'll be back in a bit."

"He traveling with any security?"

Don shook his head. "No. You know how he is. Thinks

he's got the biggest nuts in the jungle. When we were kids, our father made fun of his weight all the time, made us do push-ups. So now he compensates."

Fiona plopped on the couch, angling herself so she could keep an eye on the stairs and the large television bolted to the far wall, the latter turned to a cable news channel flashing images of a very familiar scene. "Trying to compensate is a good way to get killed. Any evil black-mailers call yet?"

"Nope. I figure they'll wait until noon, right? That was the deadline."

"Maybe. Or they might ring earlier, try and keep us on our toes." On the muted screen, the blackened remains of a large barn smoked beside a farmhouse. The image cut to what looked like an industrial pit, surrounded by forensic specialists in white jumpsuits. Fiona felt around the couch cushions for the remote, interested in what the newscaster might have to say about the small town where she and Bill almost lost their lives.

Before her hands touched anything other than scuffed leather, Don spun around with two cups of coffee in his trembling hands. "I don't know," he said, frowning as he tried to avoid spilling hot liquid everywhere. "We're not exactly pros at all this, okay? That's what we pay you for."

"Yeah, yeah." Fiona stood and liberated her coffee from his shaky grip. "When they do phone us, you're coming with me, okay?"

Don paled. "Why? We're not giving them any money."

On the television, the camera zoomed in close on a handsome FBI agent's face. Although Fiona considered her lip-reading skills subpar, she could tell when his mouth formed the words 'suspects,' 'fugitives,' and 'New York.' Wonderful. "Because they'll be suspicious if one of the famous Dusty brothers doesn't show up," she said. "I want them thinking they still got the advantage. Don't worry, I'll keep you safe. And one other thing: we're taking my car."

"Why?"

"I like how it handles. It does off-road really well, if we need it to."

"Okay."

"You got a big bag with a zipper, one you don't care about?" Fiona knew from personal experience that a half-million dollars in hundred-dollar bills weighed somewhere in the neighborhood of thirty pounds. There was a good chance that whoever arranged this blackmailing knew the right weight, too.

"Why are you rushing me?" Based on his tone, Don had decided to substitute dread for anger. "We got like three hours before they call…"

A phone beside the coffee-makers buzzed, jolting Don hard enough to spatter coffee on his hands. Fiona checked her watch, sensing it was showtime.

4

BILL HAD HIS passport, his hotel key-card, and a hundred in Cuban pesos. The money would last him hardly any time at all on the street, unless he started pickpocketing tourists. There was also the Piaget Altiplano ticking on his wrist, but he would never part with his favorite timepiece. Not after all the blood and thunder he had endured to keep it.

Tucked in the cool, dark womb of El Floridita, he downed his third daiquiri and reviewed his options. The blonde lady beside him, dressed in denim shorts and a T-shirt with the Cuban flag on it, seemed like a convenient target: her leather bag hung from the back of her seat, unzipped.

At this early hour, only a few tourists occupied the round red tables along the wall. The crimson-vested bartender—distracted, tired, or maybe hungover—ran a rag along the lacquered shelf behind the bar. Nobody glanced at Bill as he leaned toward the bag, spying a folded wad of pesos and the shiny edge of a phone just inside the opening. Perfect. Go for the cash first.

Gesturing to the bartender for another drink, he pulled out his wallet—and promptly dropped it on the floor. Leaning over to retrieve it, he let his forearm brush the bag, his fingers darting inside. As he straightened, the pesos disappeared into his cupped palm.

The blonde lady, fixated on the life-size statue of Hemingway leaning on the far end of the bar, appeared none the wiser. Hells bells, Bill thought. I guess I haven't lost my skills after all. After transferring the stolen money to his jacket pocket, he turned to his freshened daiquiri and puzzled over his crisis.

He couldn't go back to the hotel right now. The lobby of the Meliá Cohíba offered visitors a wide selection of couches and chairs, most with excellent views of the doors, front desk, and elevators. The creepy couple, in their fashion-forward tourist gear, could haunt there forever without anyone bothering them.

And who's to say they didn't have his room number already? They could wait for a maid to open the door and walk in as if they belonged there, ambush Bill whenever he entered.

With a little more money, he could take a chance on the airport, buy a flight to somewhere less heavy. That would mean abandoning everything in his room: the suits, the cash, his phone, Fiona's luggage…

Fiona.

He pictured his phone tucked in his bag beside the bed, ringing nonstop, his girlfriend panicking on the other end. Why hadn't he brought it with him, or at least checked for messages before walking out the door? He knew the answer: their last fight had left him in a mood.

When the blonde lady turned to him, he tensed, ready for the accusation. Instead she smiled, flashing rows of perfect teeth, and his guts unclenched a little. She was young, maybe early twenties, her unlined face suggesting a lifetime of only trivial worries.

"Hey," she said, slurring a little. "I'm Marnie."

"Steve." He made no move to shake her hand.

Marnie leaned into him. "Where you from, Steve?"

He placed her accent in the Midwest somewhere, the vowels flat as Kansas. "Arkansas. How about you?"

She dodged the question. "We're here on educational exchange. Part of a graduate program thing." Her voice dipped to a confidential timbre. "I know they say it's dangerous to leave the group, because of crime? But I had to get a drink. Our professor's been driving us just that crazy."

"Sounds like you're having a heck of a morning."

She laughed. "Could be worse, I guess. Can I ask you something weird?"

"Sure."

She nodded at the statue. "That's Ernest Heming-way, right?"

"Uh, yeah." Bill jabbed a finger at the wall behind the bronze figure. "See that photo above his head, to the left a bit? That's Hemingway and Castro. He used to live down here. As a kid I used to read all his stuff, loved it. Even 'To

Have and Have Not,' although I think I'm the only one who does. Have you read it?"

"No, he's too macho for my taste." Her face scrunched, in the way of drunk people trying to concentrate on reality, and she gestured at Bill's raised hand. "I'm sorry, I shouldn't ask, but how did you lose…"

He turned his wrist, giving her a better view of the index finger, which ended in a scarred stump at the second knuckle. "A crooked cop chopped it off because I wouldn't tell him where the money was."

"You're kidding."

"Nope." He wiggled the stump. "Don't worry, though. Once I broke free, I shot him."

Her smile died. "No, tell me you're kidding."

"Nope. I got the drop on him because he slipped on my severed finger. I'm in Cuba because I'm a wanted man back in the States."

Her hands flattened on the bar, her legs stiffening. She was about to leave, and that was a problem, because he needed her phone if he wanted to stay alive. Working every ounce of warmth he could into a broad grin, he said: "Got you."

Marnie's lips twitched upwards. "Really?"

"Yeah. Severed in a car accident. No big deal. I mean, it was a big deal at the time, don't get me wrong, but I'm sort of used to it now."

She relaxed into her seat. "You're weird."

He saluted her with his glass. "What'd you expect in a bar at this hour?"

"No, not weird in a bad way. Just different." She

skimmed a strand of hair away from her face. "So you're a tourist? You here alone?"

Bill took the opportunity to bend closer, his hand on the back of her chair. He could smell the rum and lime on her breath. "I'm on a Hemingway tour. Told you I was a fan, remember? We see his house, pet the cats, all that jazz."

"Petting the cats sounds macho." She gestured at her empty glass. "I think I need another drink. I can't face the idea of heading back to the hotel quite yet."

"I'll get it." Bill's hand disappeared into his jacket.

"Thanks." Marnie stood, slinging her bag onto her shoulder. "And I have to hit the loo. Be right back."

Once she disappeared around the corner, Bill leaned back in his seat, flexing his fingers like a pianist after a long concert. Always a little paranoid about his health, he wondered if the ache in his bones was the first sign of arthritis. Her stolen phone sat heavy in his jacket pocket, beside her cash.

You're slick, boy! Still got it!

Slipping another few pesos onto the bar, he stood and headed for the door, his feet only a little unsteady. You want another sign you're ancient? When you can't down copious amounts of alcohol with no ill effects. I got to retire, he thought.

The bright Havana sun smacked him full in the face. Pausing at the curb to allow a few bright junkers to cruise past, he pulled out Marnie's phone and flicked the power button. The device ran an older version of Android he could crack, provided he had enough time. Pocketing it again, he crossed the road, intending to disappear into Havana's grungy Chinatown for a few hours.

Marnie shouted behind him.

So much for being slick. She must have wanted to check her Facebook in the bathroom, or something.

Bill forced himself to walk at a normal pace. *Find a cab, get the hell out of here.* A half-block away, a pair of teenagers tucked beneath the open hood of a cherry-red Ford, banging on the engine with a wrench wrapped in tape. When one of them paused and turned around, Bill caught his eye and raised his hands to grip an invisible wheel.

The kid started to nod, only to jolt upright and tap his friend's shoulder. They slammed the hood and ducked into the car, which squealed away from the curb fast enough to leave a black comma of burnt rubber behind.

That was odd. Who around here turned down a chance at cold, hard cash?

Bill risked a glance behind him.

Oh.

A cop stood in front of the bar, a hand on his sidearm. Marnie gripped his elbow while spinning a tale of deception and thievery in what sounded like pitch-perfect Spanish. The cop asked a question, and she waved an arm at Bill.

Shit.

While dressing that morning, Bill had selected a pair of Berluti calfskin loafers, hand-stitched and sleek and totally unfit for running. The slick soles squeaked on the pavement as he sprinted through the crowds, praying that the law would hesitate at the prospect of tackling a tourist long enough to give him even the most pathetic head-start. His beautiful hat flew off, disappearing into a gap between two parked cars. In the reflection of a startled bystander's sunglasses he saw the distorted shape of the policeman in pursuit, firearm free of its holster, Marnie hard on his heels. Ankles already screaming in pain, Bill tried to accelerate, his panicked breath loud in his ears.

THE CALLER TOLD them to drive into the hills, take a certain road to a clearing. Fiona and Don piled into the jeep and headed off, saying nothing as the bright colors and chipped concrete of town gave way to grassy slopes, barbed-wire fences, and the occasional brick house. Along the dusty shoulder of the road, workers walked in single file, waving whenever Fiona tooted the horn.

"What'd you put in there?" Don said, nodding at the soiled duffel bag in the backseat.

"About twenty pounds of tobacco, but don't worry, no leaves, just the little bits. I asked the sweepers to give me the scraps."

Don laughed. "A couple years back, we tried taking those scraps, making cigarettes out of them. They sold, but not enough. You can't fight Big Tobacco."

"You know what's a good rule for life?" Fiona said. "Don't fight groups dedicated to killing millions of people."

"That's hilarious." Don fumbled beneath his shirt and drew a silver .32-caliber pistol from his waistband, waving it at the ceiling like a bandit on a drunken rampage. "By the way, I brought this. You know, just in case. Better safe than sorry."

Fiona resisted the urge to snatch the pistol out of his hand and toss it out the window. Mostly because the road had transitioned into a series of dusty switchbacks, and she needed to focus on steering. "Wonderful," she said through gritted teeth. "You have a gun. You ever shoot that before, champ?"

"I'll have you know our father taught us to shoot. I'm pretty good. No expert marksman, but I can sure hit a target."

"Do me a favor: put that away before you blow your balls off," she snapped.

Don let his pistol sag between his knees. "Fine."

"Now do me a second favor: pull out your phone, and check how many ways we can get back to town other than on this road."

"I think this is the only way. Trust me, I've lived here for years."

"I want to see what Google says."

With a shrug, Don slipped the pistol into his jeans and pulled his phone from his pocket. After tapping and pinching the screen, he frowned. "I told you, it's just this one."

She took her eyes off the road long enough to look at the screen. "Crap."

"Doesn't mean there's not another way back down, dirt or something, but it's not showing up on here. As far as Goo-gle's concerned, this road is it."

"We'll have to make the best of things." Her thoughts drifted to that news clip of the barn in flames, and the FBI agent talking about fugitives. How do you make the best of things when everybody in the world wants a piece of you?

"I think we're close." Don pointed through the windshield. Straight ahead, the road terminated in a tangle of rocks and greenery. The cliff to their right offered a panoramic view of Estelí's ragged grid of red roofs, softened by the morning haze. On their left, through a gap in the scrawny trees, a narrow dirt lane led into a glade stippled in shadow.

"I guess so," Fiona said, turning down the lane. After five yards she slammed on the brakes.

"What? What's wrong?" Flailing Don scrambled for his waistband, head thrashing as he tried to locate the threat.

"Nothing yet," Fiona said, throwing the jeep into reverse. "Just setting us up." One hand on the wheel, she executed a deft three-point turn that left the vehicle angled toward the road. In the rearview mirror, she saw a shirtless boy in a muddy dirt-bike helmet step into the clearing, the fractured sunlight through the trees flashing off something metallic in his hand.

"Don?" Fiona said, shutting off the engine.

"Yeah?"

"I want you to take a breath and hold it."

Don let his head flop forward, inhaling through his nose. "Good," Fiona said. "Now exhale slowly. Count to ten in your head as you do it."

Don obeyed. When the last of the air left his lungs, he inhaled again and asked: "Why am I doing this?"

"Feeling relaxed?"

He grinned. "A little, sure?"

Fiona gripped her door handle. "Good. There's a kid with a gun right behind us, and I don't want you losing your shit like a little girl."

Don lost his shit like a little girl. While he flailed in his seat, Fiona opened the rear hatch of the jeep and fetched the duffel bag. The jungle air wrapped her head like a sauna towel, her forehead instantly beaded with sweat.

The kid stopped in the middle of the glade, cheap pistol loose in his grip, finger off the trigger. Fiona decided to meet him there, tall grass slapping against her calves. She made a big show of wrestling with the bag's weight. She wanted the kid to take it and hold it close.

When she came within fifteen feet, the kid raised a hand, palm out. She stopped and asked: *"Habla inglés?"*

The kid shook his head and pointed over his shoulder at the forest, where a second man emerged from the trees: white, older, his gray hair shorn in a tight crew cut, his arm muscles bulging like stones in a leather bag. He wore a black bullet-resistant vest over a gray T-shirt, and jeans. A black .45 automatic dangled in the holster on his hip.

"Oh crap," Fiona said, her pistol drawn and raised before the second word left her mouth.

Crew Cut lifted his arms and smiled, seemingly unconcerned about the prospect of a bullet in his brain.

"Been a long time, dear. When's the last time I saw you? That night in Newark, the thing with the pen?"

Her weapon aimed at his forehead, Fiona considered taking the shot. Quarter-second for the pull, then shift to the kid if he tried to draw down. After that, hit the dirt and crawl back to the jeep, in case other shooters lurked in the woods. Through the trees she glimpsed—or imagined she glimpsed—the white flank and tinted windows of a large SUV, although the light out here played tricks with your mind..

The dry click of a pistol-hammer behind her. She risked a look back. Don stood beside the jeep, his .32 aimed squarely at her back. His cheeks bloodless, the pistol wavering only a little.

"Your luck's run out." Crew Cut mock-apologetic as he crept for her. "But did you really expect any different? From the very beginning, you must have known how this would end."

"There was no blackmail, was there?" Fiona, you idiot.

Crew Cut shook his head. "The Dean had a great idea: set up a fake job, lure you out."

"I'm sorry, Fiona," Don called out, his voice quaking.

"I'm going to chop your balls off," Fiona yelled over her shoulder. "You and your brother."

The kid gestured for the duffel bag, and with a shrug Fiona tossed it at his feet. He hefted the strap onto his shoulder, the bag angled toward Crew Cut. Good.

"Bill's not with me," Fiona said.

"Oh, I know," Crew Cut said. "He's in Havana. We have two people on him now."

And Bill's not much of a fighter, whispered that voice

in Fiona's head. Sure, he can take care of himself, but not against two killers. Not in a place where we don't have friends.

Crew Cut began to lower his arms. The kid, standing near him, fumbled one-handed with the bag's zipper. Something clanked.

Fiona chuckled. "Good thing I believed this was blackmail."

His hands level with his ribs—low enough to make a play for his holster—Crew Cut smirked at her, probably expecting a joke. "Yeah? Why's that?"

A hard tug, and the bag unzipped.

Fiona squeezed her eyes shut.

The blackness inside her eyelids exploded nuclear red. The bang smacked her eardrums hard as fists, dropping her to one knee.

Over the apocalyptic ringing in her ears, she heard a high-pitched scream. She opened her eyes again. The world was a squirmy purple octopus. She blinked her overloaded retinas clear. The kid danced shrieking for the trees, the skin on his right side black with ash, bits of flaming bag and tobacco scorching his helmet. Crew Cut stumbled in the other direction, hands pressed to his ears, mouth open in a silent howl.

Fiona took the opportunity to lift her pistol and fire one, two, three times, aiming for the head-shot but hitting Crew Cut center-mass as he swiveled, a pink spray as a bullet found meat. He dropped out of sight. Without pausing, she spun to the jeep, ready to put a bullet in Don before he put one in her.

Don had already dropped his pistol. Over her

gunsights Fiona had a prime angle on his skinny ass as he ripped open his passenger door. Her next bullet, aimed at his knees, only skimmed his left hip, shredding the leg of his jeans. Yelping Don plowed headfirst into the glove compartment before flopping out of the vehicle and onto the grass, thrashing as he clutched his bleeding nose with both hands.

Fiona scrambled to him and leveled her smoking pistol an inch from his forehead. Her ears had settled enough to hear him gurgling in pain. "Flash-bangs," she yelled. "Friend gave 'em to me."

Don howled something that might have been *"what"* or *"shit."* His pulped nose made it hard to tell.

"Come on." She shoved him hard against the side of the jeep, reaching into the back pocket of her jeans for the riot cuffs. It was hard to lasso his wrists while holding the gun, but she had some experience with this sort of thing. With his hands bound at the waist, and his nose freely pouring red, she pushed him into the passenger seat.

As she slammed the passenger door, the jeep's back window exploded in a glittering spray of safety glass. She ducked and spun, glimpsing Crew Cut's head as he dove beneath the grass. Pacing off her shots, she retreated around the front of the jeep, using its bulk as a shield, until she reached the driver's door and yanked it open. Sliding into the seat like a normal person would have made a nice target of her silhouetted head, so she flopped inside on her stomach, stabbed the key in the ignition, shifted into drive, and pressed down the gas pedal with her hand.

The windshield coughed glass, two small holes appearing above the steering wheel. Don yelped. The jeep rolled slowly down the dirt lane, picking up speed as gas and gravity did their work, and she tucked her legs onto the seat. The open driver's door banged against a small tree, slamming it shut against her heels. She risked peeking over the dashboard, gripping the wheel in both hands as she did so.

"*I'b sobby,*" Don blubbered, his chin a mess of blood and drool. "*Sobby, tho sobby.*"

"Better duck," Fiona said. The rearview mirror framed Crew Cut in a classic two-handed shooter's stance, his shoulder above the black vest soaked red, not that the damage spoiled the steadiness of his aim.

Don's head flopped forward, speckling the dashboard with blood from his nose, as Crew Cut's next shot hit something in the jeep's rear that responded with a loud boom. The wheel turned traitor, burning her palms, and she tried to steer into the slide as best she could, but the jeep was too close to the edge of the cliff.

They went over.

Through the windshield she saw sky, trees, sky again.

Fiona's stomach dropped.

Don shrieked.

The jeep skidded broadside down the slope, its wheels spinning great plumes of dirt and rocks, branches slapping the windshield. Fiona tried to control the descent, steer away from the larger boulders, only to have the vehicle tilt hard on two wheels, inches from toppling over. Don screeched in harmony with crumpling steel. Through the trees she saw a flash, maybe sun on glass, and they crashed through a screen of thorny shrubs into the shanty.

The jeep plowed through the first shack clean, wooden boards bouncing off the cracking windshield, boom, chickens flapping scared in her path, a plastic barrel crushed beneath her wheels as the bumper missed a rusty stove by inches, boom, an instant of sunlight before they plowed into the next house down the hill, a loose lump of clothing smacking the hood making her think oh God she hit someone maybe a child but it was only laundry thank God, the jeep demolishing a mattress in an explosion of springs and stuffing before smashing through a tin wall, boom, bouncing off a flat boulder hard enough to send her throat hard against the seat belt, choking, blood trickling down her face as she slammed against the steering wheel, the ceiling, the window that broke under the force of her elbow sending a fresh jolt of pain up her arm but she could still grip the wheel not that it did much good as the jeep ruined yet another shanty-house a chicken splattering the crumpled hood leaving a dark fan of blood some poor family's livelihood, shit, bouncing off a log and airborne weightless about to vomit—

The jeep crashed onto a paved road, engine grinding, headlights shattered, the paint scratched away, the hood peeled like the lid of a used can.

Good thing I used that fake name with the rental agency, Fiona thought, otherwise I might be in some real trouble here. That was before she spied, through the gummy mess of the broken windshield, something that made her erupt into hysterics: a tattered bra, with faded flowers on its cups, wrapped around the top of the jeep's antenna like the flag of a lunatic pirate.

Someone hollered above them, and her laughter

died. Halfway up the hill, an older woman stood on the wooden platform that had once been her house, unleashing a torrent of curses.

Fiona ran shaking hands over her body for wounds. A few cuts on her hands and forehead, a deeper gash on her wrist, otherwise nothing serious. Lodged between her thighs, a severed chicken head glared at her.

"Sorry, little dude," she said, and the chicken head blinked.

Beside her, Don clutched his leg and wept softly.

"Don." Fiona searched the trashed interior for her pistol, finding it wedged between her seat and the middle console. Prying the weapon free, she engaged the safety and slipped it back in her holster. Even if Crew Cut had a car handy in that glade, she doubted he felt suicidal enough to drive down the cliff after them, and taking the switchbacks would require a few minutes.

Don looked at her, his cheeks wet with sweat and tears, his lips a tight white line.

"You told me once you chartered planes," she asked, trying to keep her voice level as her stomach lurched. "Can you get one? Like right now?"

He moaned deep in his throat, and she felt an absurd pity for him. Then she remembered his betrayal, and the feeling passed. Leaning across the seats, she pinched his ear and bent it toward her. "Earth to Don," she whispered. "Come in, Don."

He sniffed as his brain returned from its interstellar journey. "*Yeb*," he said, before pausing to swallow. His breath whistling through his damaged nose, he tried to enunciate more clearly: "Managua. The airport. We *hab* our share of it, pay maintenance, but we *habn't uthed* it in a long time. Cost-cutting…"

"Spare me. We're going there, after we make a stop." Fiona fed some gas to the engine, which responded by whining louder. The wheels inched forward. With a little luck, they might make it to Estelí, although luck was in short supply lately.

Don rubbed his bound wrists together and said: "Doctor."

"How about a Cuban doctor?" Fiona said, pushing their deathtrap vehicle faster. "I hear they're the best."

Don shut his eyes as Fiona navigated the broken jeep toward town. She prayed no cop would pull them over. Her dream image returned, of Bill floating in the dark ocean, his skin food for fish. She tried to send him a psychic message across time and distance: I'm coming, baby. Don't do anything too stupid until I get there.

In the skewed rearview mirror, a white SUV bounced into view, spraying dust as it took the curve hard.

6

ONLY THE DUMBEST of luck saved Bill in his flight from the cop. At the first intersection, in defiance of gravity and his aging muscles, he vaulted over the hood of a pink Ford sedan. The driver, startled by the body flying past, accidentally stomped on the gas—and plowed into the officer pursuing Bill. Three tons of antique Detroit steel sent the poor bastard flying into the air.

Marnie stopped in her tracks and screamed.

Bill kept running, the meaty hard drive in his skull cycling up memories of a hundred chases through the streets of New York: times he dodged, times he chased. What worked, or left him broken and covered in blood. In this case, the penalty for failure was prison in a country with precious little concept of the words 'due process.'

A few blocks later, with no pursuers in sight, Bill

slowed his stride and ducked into a dusty gift store. The brown husk of a proprietor regarded him with suspicion as he paused near a wooden shelf stacked with neatly folded T-shirts. Bill bent down, his hands on his knees, concentrating on deep breaths. When he stood again, he pulled the wad of bills out of his pocket, and the proprietor softened a bit.

Yes, the T-shirt he bought featured the glowering face of Ernesto 'Che' Guevara. Bill often wondered how the world's hippest guerilla revolutionary would have felt about all the capitalist dollars earned on his image over the years. He also purchased shorts with the Cuban flag stitched on the left leg, another existential puzzle of commercialism and branding that he would need to work out over several glasses of something high-proof. A new baseball cap and a pair of rubber sandals completed the disguise; his watch, far too expensive to wear on his exposed wrist without drawing attention, went into his pocket along with his passport and hotel key-card.

His lungs still burning from the run, Bill walked the narrow streets a few blocks east of El Capitolio. Bystanders kept glancing at the beautiful suit and shirt balled under his arm, his nice shoes dangling from his hand. You're going to have to do something about the clothes, he told himself. They're attracting too much attention in a place where nobody earns anything.

In the three weeks that Bill and Fiona had stayed in Havana, neither had wandered into this part of town. The elegant facades and curving archways reminded him a little of Paris, although decades of sea air and neglect had sanded away the detailing and color. Everything was peeling and crumbling, ghostly in the tropical sunlight. The residents on the rusted balconies regarded him coolly as he passed.

At the end of one street, he found an apartment building reduced to a shell, its walls choked with vines. He ducked through the open doorway and climbed over piles of rubble until he stood in the bright and roofless center of the space. Setting the suit on a flat chunk of brickwork, he pulled out his borrowed phone and powered it up. A solid four bars of signal. Good.

The Android operating system is the most popular in the world, with good reason: any manufacturer can load it onto their devices without paying a fee to Google, which developed it. Dozens of types of phones run Android, and the carriers that connect those devices to the world often fail to update the software on a regular basis. No matter how smart the people who created it, older operating systems have flaws, some of which Bill had memorized in the course of his hustling life.

Holding down the phone's power and volume buttons forced a reset. When the screen revived, a message box asked if Bill wanted to activate 'Recovery Mode.' More button-pushes, and a few screens later, he had the option of deleting all of Marnie's data. "I'm sorry," he told his drinking buddy in absentia, and fried her precious info.

The phone, now cleansed, rebooted. As it ran in setup mode, Bill held his breath, praying that it would start up without too many complications. A cheerful Welcome screen bloomed to life and asked for his Google ID, which he gratefully provided. The home-screen appeared, followed by a message bubble from Fiona: "Bill?"

According to the time-stamp, she had sent the text last night. Was she still angry? Or just worried?

"In trouble," he texted back. "They found us."

Hitting send, he slipped the phone into his pocket, retrieved his bundle of clothes, and exited the ruin. Up the street, a group of kids jumped and splashed in the spray from a burst pipe, yelling with such joy it made Bill smile despite his worries.

He headed for his hotel, plotting a path through the neighborhoods that would swing him wide of El Floridita. Every so often, he noted a police car cruising in the distance, usually a Peugeot 106 with white detailing that made it easy to pick out amidst the browns and grays of the crumbling buildings. He was on the lookout for a specific kind of bystander, and found him in the shadow of a Stalinist apartment tower, a five-story concrete cube enlivened by an aquamarine paint-job badly in need of a touch-up. Or rather, the man found him.

"Cigars? Good price."

Bill turned, sizing up his questioner: scrawny, dressed in an old shirt and a loose pair of slacks that, like the buildings around him, had seen much better days. He had a scraggly beard that would have done the Fathers of the Revolution proud, and a faded baseball cap. Best of all, he was roughly Bill's height.

"*Habla inglés?*" Bill asked.

The man waggled his hand. "A little, *si*."

I'm having all the luck today, Bill thought. "No cigars," he said, and flashed a tight roll of pesos. "I have a job, though. *Dinero, si?*"

The man stepped back. "*Si?*"

"Quick job," Bill said. "How do you say that, *rápido*?"

The wind had picked up, hurling massive waves against the seawall of the Malecón. Heavy spray doused the walkway and the road. The gutters had a hard time swallowing down that water, and cars surfed through the deepening puddles with suicidal sangfroid, sometimes skidding out of control. The waves also cleared away the pedestrians, and thus any witnesses.

Fiona had texted him back. "Things went wrong here," she wrote. "Heading your way."

Whenever Fiona, the master of understatement, said that things had gone wrong, that probably meant a stack of dead bodies and a couple of buildings on fire.

"I think it's Rockaway," he texted back.

"Yes. Ran into old friend," she wrote. "Still after us."

Time to run again, Bill thought. Where should we go this time? Where *can* we go, with the money we have left? Despite his reputation as a spendthrift, Bill would curb his splurging if forced to do so; but even then, their savings would only last a few more months. Living as a fugitive meant burning cash on everything from safe houses to ammunition, with precious little opportunity to stop in any one place and earn more.

A few blocks from the Meliá Cohíba, a secondary road paralleled the Malecón, lined on either side with tall apartment buildings. It could have been Miami, if you squinted a little. With the wind had come clouds, darkening the sky to a premature dusk. The cars that deviated onto this road to avoid the waves had their headlights on.

In the dimmer light, the man in the white suit

glimmered like a specter. He ambled down that side road, hands in his pockets, a baseball cap tucked low on his forehead. At the intersection he angled left, toward the rear of the hotel. You could probably see him from the lobby, if you sat on a couch with a good view through the windows.

Two blocks behind the man wearing his suit, Bill ducked from parked car to parked car, shadow to shadow, his calfskin loafers still in hand. Even if he lost his beautiful seersucker, which was looking damn likely at this juncture, at least he had saved his shoes. When his hustler friend disappeared behind the hotel, Bill accelerated, keeping his eyes locked on the front driveway. A doorman bent to speak through the open window of a cab idling at the curb, but otherwise the world was empty.

Then, the couple.

They drifted out of the black doorway of the Meliá Cohíba like ghosts, shoulder to shoulder. They wore the same clothes as when Bill had spotted them on the Malecón, their hands still deep in their pockets. They took a left at the bottom of the driveway and floated toward the rear of the building. Bill hoped his new friend had taken his advice and started running once he passed the hotel, but maybe things had gotten lost in translation.

Once the couple disappeared from view, Bill trotted across the intersection and into the lobby, offering the doorman a quick nod as he did so. Tourists clustered around the couches and chairs, along with a crew of giant men in sunglasses and cargo pants. Their T-shirts bore the logo of a popular film franchise in which a group of beautiful people traveled around the world racing expensive cars and robbing banks. Bill remembered that the government had shut down portions of the Malecón for two days so that a pair of Ferraris could engage in a simulated chase across a couple miles of crumbling infrastructure.

"Freedom," Bill announced to nobody as he ducked into the elevator, slipping his key-card into the slot that would gain him access to the higher floors. Despite the full lobby, he was alone in here. Only when the doors slid shut did he exhale, loudly, and lean against the softly vibrating wall of the car. He felt like he could sleep for a week.

Pulling out his phone, he texted: "Hotel not safe."

No response. Was she on a plane? Still in Nicaragua? He hadn't felt this scared since Oklahoma, when he lost his finger. It was the sort of dread that grew in your stomach until it was a heavy mass that threatened to drag you down to the floor. You could squeeze your hands into fists and breathe deep to keep your nerves under control, and maybe that would help for a few minutes, but Bill knew the only real solution was to escape the threat as soon as possible.

The doors hissed open, the car bobbing in that disconcerting way of elevators in need of new parts. Ducking his head into the hallway, he checked in both directions before stepping out. Their room was two doors to the right, the black plastic 'Por Favor, No Molestar' sign still on the knob.

It felt like a century since he'd left. His duffel lay open on the bed, piled high with clothes. Stripping off his obnoxious T-shirt and shorts, he wiped himself down with a towel still moist from his morning shower. The sprint in his expensive shoes had left his feet reddened, two toenails cracked and bleeding. He bandaged the wounds as best he could from Fiona's small medical kit on the sink and returned to the bedroom to dress.

He chose a blue button-down from the closet and paired it with a summer wool suit, gray, his favorite. His passport went in his right pants pocket, his cash and cards in the left, a last Bolivar cigar inside his jacket. Slipping his watch back onto his left wrist made him feel complete.

The loss of his white seersucker reduced his luggage by roughly a third, making it easy to stuff the rest of his underwear, designer jeans, and shirts into the duffel. His phone buzzed: a message from Fiona: "Inbound this eve. Meet at spot?"

Instead of replying, Bill opened the closet and retrieved Fiona's canvas overnighter. His lady had mastered the art of traveling light, mostly because she refused to wear anything other than jeans and a rotating collection of T-shirts. Shouldering both bags, he walked across the room, testing the heft and balance. It felt awkward, clumsy.

The phone hummed again: "Forget bags. Just take what matters."

"Baby, you know me too well," he said to the empty room.

He had no intention of giving up his duffel, a buffalo-leather number he had picked up in Nassau the day after they escaped their hosts in the Dominican Republic, or any of his remaining clothes. I'll just tell her my bag had more room, and that's why I had to abandon hers. Besides, didn't she want to buy a new one, anyway?

Finding a loose thread on the bottom of Fiona's bag, he yanked. The seam split, revealing a secret space between the inner and outer walls. Cash tumbled onto the bed, along with a fresh set of credit cards and Fiona's spare passport.

Tossing those goodies atop his clothes, he tapped out a message on his phone, telling Fiona where to meet. After hitting the Send key, he paused, transfixed by the image of her emerging from the misty jungle like an avenging goddess, her eyes blazing hellfire through a dirt-crusted face, her skin speckled and smeared with mud and gunpowder. Ready to hurt someone. Especially someone who neglected to provide her with fresh underwear.

Before he zipped his bag closed, he slipped in a pair of her panties, a bra, and a clean T-shirt.

It's the little things that keep a relationship alive.

Onto the next task: exiting the building with his throat and balls intact. Had the gruesome twosome returned to the lobby, or were they still pursuing his suit across Havana? He hoped that hustler had given them the slip. Either way, he needed to take a service exit—after he armed himself appropriately.

Wrapping the Che T-shirt around his fist, he entered the bathroom.

7

FIONA AND CREW cut went way back.

Crew Cut had always told her that his name was William Bonney, but Fiona saw right through that bull-crap. His haircut, his orderliness, and the way he moved suggested a military background, so Crew Cut fit as well as any other name that Fiona could have given him. She did believe his stories about serving in Iraq as a contractor, banging it out with insurgents on dusty streets and rooftops, but only because she had seen him in action on more than one job. He was dangerous.

And he was right behind her.

In its crippled state, her jeep had a hard time accelerating. Steam whisped from the crumpled hood, and the wheel shuddered in her hands. In the passenger seat,

Don groaned every time the vehicle hit a bump, his nose swollen to clownish dimensions.

The white SUV lurked twenty feet behind her, trapped in place by a rattling red jalopy that looked worse for wear than her jeep, if you could believe it. Through the SUV's windshield, she saw Crew Cut hunched over the wheel. No way to tell how much damage her bullet had done to his shoulder.

Fiona stuck an arm out her window and offered him a hearty thumbs-up. After the punishing ride down the hill, even that simple gesture sent bolts of pain shooting into her chest. Nothing felt broken, and she had none of the chills or shakes that came with internal bleeding, but her skin would probably look like a purple blanket come morning.

Crew Cut responded with a middle finger. So much for civility.

"How you feeling?" Fiona asked Don.

Don wheezed something about his face ruined forever.

"Think of all the chicks you'll pick up with the scars," Fiona said. Ahead of them loomed a school bus painted in swirls of bright color, its roof loaded with bags. She eased the jeep into the oncoming lane, judging traffic, and decided it was time to make her move. Provided, of course, that her wheezing, coughing, shuddering, *dying* engine held out long enough.

Fiona floored it. The jeep's choked snarl rose to a high-pitched shriek, its frame shimmying. A truck loomed in her shattered windshield, its horn blaring. She veered back into her own lane, in front of the bus, with only a few feet to spare.

With that daredevil maneuver, she increased her lead over the white SUV by a hundred yards. A quick right sent her off the main road and onto a side-street, a cloud of dust marking her path like a flag. The yellow front of the coffin store appeared, the owner's daughter sitting in its open doorway.

Ten seconds later, the white SUV screeched through the intersection, almost hitting two dirt-bikes, and braked at the head of the dirt alley that ran behind the coffin shop, blocking in the battered jeep parked beside the rear door. Crew Cut scuttled out low, pistol in his left hand, his right shoulder moist and red above his vest. His forehead slick, his cheeks pale, but his eyes clear and cold.

Keeping low, Crew Cut angled around the jeep. Empty seats, keys in the ignition, a chicken head in the foot-well. He hissed. He turned to the door that led into the coffin shop.

The first floor was dim. He crouched in the doorway while his vision adjusted, then swept through the only room, lined on either side with cheap coffins on wooden platforms. The open front door framed the girl on the steps, who twisted around to watch him. He raised a hand for her to stay quiet, wincing at the pain flaring up his shoulder.

Crew Cut reached for the lid of the nearest coffin, ready to play whack-a-mole, when something thumped overhead. It sounded like a heavy footstep.

Offering the girl a tight smile, he moved left, where a narrow stairway led to the second floor. He took the risers slow, ready for Fiona to try something, his whole world reduced to the view over his barrel. She was a tricky one, that lady. Not so great when it came to picking men, but a damn virtuoso with a Kalashnikov.

At the top of the stairs, he faced a closed wooden door. Taking a deep breath, he drove a foot into the knob, shattering it, and ducked into the next room. His pistol swept over a few pieces of cheap furniture, an empty floor, an unmade bed.

He tiptoed to the window. The adjoining rooftop was flat and empty. Over his pounding heartbeat, and the hum of cars below, he noticed another sound: the steady patter of a shower on low. It came from behind the only other door in the room.

Crew Cut hesitated. Who turned on the shower in the middle of a chase? Or had Fiona hid downstairs, leaving him to blunder like some idiot into a stranger's apartment?

Instead of wasting time thinking over this dilemma, Crew Cut put two bullets into the bathroom door, just in case that bitch was waiting behind it. Sly boys stay alive, as he always liked to say. The door drifted open, framing a red-tiled bathroom with a shower stall in one corner. The shower spat water onto a small pile of cracked tile and grouting left by his bullets.

He entered the bathroom. No bodies in a corner, no blood, no signs of a gun or broken glass or any of the other things you shed when you're injured after driving a car off a cliff.

From behind him came the click of wood on wood.

What felt like a sledgehammer hit him between the shoulder blades. He heard the dry crack of a gunshot. His knees sagged, dipping him headfirst into the shower stall.

What happens when electrified water meets flesh?

Nothing good.

Fiona slid from the crawl-space beneath the floorboards, smoking pistol in hand, in time to see Crew Cut trembling and twitching against the drain, the water swirling pink from the wound in his shoulder. His boots hammered a hard beat against the tiles.

There was no way that plan should have worked. She knew Crew Cut was the kind of killer who took his time, swept each room before moving onto the next. That bought her a full minute to turn on the shower, pry up the floorboards, and tuck beneath. It was a half-assed plan, but she was too injured to face him in the open and live.

Fiona sighted the pistol on his head.

Her hands began to shake. As if the electricity had somehow shot out of the shower stall and across the floor and into her body through the soles of her shoes.

She braced her gun wrist with her other hand.

Just a case of nerves or something.

A low growl in her throat, her jaw tightening.

Her finger steadied on the trigger.

The next bullet finished things.

Shivering Don flinched like a vampire at dawn when she raised the lid of the coffin where she had placed him before running upstairs. "Time to go, Lazarus," she said, her ears still ringing from gunfire, the comforting weight of the money-bag on her shoulder.

On the way to the jeep, she handed a thousand dollars to the owner's daughter. It made her feel a little better about leaving a body behind. Crew Cut wouldn't have to travel far for his coffin.

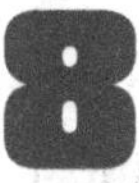

FIONA HARBORED A deep hatred of flying. Turbulence, no matter how slight, always drove her into a feral panic. Over the years she had read dozens of articles proclaiming the safety of air travel, and the infinitesimal chances of dying in a wreck, and yet the roar of plane engines still made her lizard brain queue up an inflight mind-movie of exploding fuselages and bodies.

Ever think you'll win the lottery? Bill once asked her during takeoff, as she clutched his fingers hard enough to make him wince.

No, she replied. *It's an idiot tax.*

So why do you think you'll die in a crash? Bill smiled. *It's even higher odds.*

She had leaned over and kissed his cheek, more for his

benefit than hers. Those mind-movies continued to play: fireballs, screaming, death.

Before leaving Estelí, Fiona and Don stopped at the cigar factory. Don's house, a two-story block of rough concrete and big windows, stood at the far edge of the parking lot, beyond a high fence. It took him forever to find his keys and passport. They traded up the wrecked jeep for Don's aging BMW, which stank of old tobacco and feet.

Fiona put Don behind the wheel for the trip to Managua. They said almost nothing to each other, although she sensed him relaxing a little more with each passing mile. She prayed to whatever God watched over killers and outlaws that his talk about a plane would result in something other than an old Cessna stuck together with duct tape and baling wire.

They made a single stop on the way, so Fiona could strip down the pistol and toss the parts over a bridge railing. She had purchased the weapon in Managua and kept it hidden in a storage locker between trips, but it had outlived its usefulness.

"You stay calm the rest of this trip," she told Don as they approached the airport, "and you'll get through this, okay? Act up, or say the wrong thing to someone, and this gets messier than it needs to be."

Don nodded and wiped at the snot leaking from his busted nose.

At the private-jet terminal, Don filled out the appropriate paperwork while Fiona helped herself to a steaming cup of coffee from the urn on a nearby table. There were no other passengers in the small lounge, no awkward glances or questions about her bruised arms and cut face. She hoped this ride was smoother than going commercial. How often did millionaires die in plane crashes?

Their gleaming white jet came with a pair of pilots in uniforms and aviator glasses, standing on the tarmac with their hands behind their backs. "Passports?" one asked as Fiona and Don approached.

Fiona handed over her best fake one, followed by Don's real deal. The senior pilot gave their documents a perfunctory read before glancing at the bag slung under Fiona's arm. She thought he might ask her to open it up. Instead he grinned and said: "How much does that weigh?"

"I'm sorry?"

The pilot raised a hand in apology. "Sorry, weak joke. We have to determine weight before we fly, but that bag is fine." She could sense him evaluating their galaxy of scrapes and bruises.

"Oh," Fiona said. Silly rabbit, bag searches are for the peons who line up for a flying cattle-car. She felt naked without a firearm, but there was always the knife in her belt.

Once the pilots entered the cockpit and closed the door behind them, Fiona turned to Don and said: "I think this might do nicely." Although the plane cabin was tight quarters, the leather seats along the port side were plush, and the small galley across from the bathroom offered a variety of snacks. A small screen embedded in the bulkhead flickered to life, displaying a digital map of Nicaragua and the surrounding countries, with a little plane icon representing their location.

"We *ged—get*—twelve hours a month." When he spoke

slowly, and took care to enunciate every syllable, he sounded almost normal. "Too expensive, but my brother insists that we keep it." Don buckled himself into a seat and sighed. "Medkit, *pleath*."

"Where?"

"Galley."

The bottom drawer of the galley held a white plastic box with a red cross on the lid. Fiona handed it over before resuming her search for food. The cabinets yielded crackers and cookies, but no bags of barbeque chips, her personal favorite. She craved the comfort of salt and fat, a little reward for her aching body.

The intercom clicked to life. "Take your seats, please," the pilot said.

Fiona grabbed a small box of animal crackers and a bag of whole walnuts, along with a silver nutcracker from a drawer, before taking her seat nearest the door. The engines cycled to a throaty rumble, the cabin swaying gently as the plane eased forward. Fiona felt her pulse accelerate, her palms already slick with sweat.

Don smiled. "Hate flying?"

Fiona nodded.

The smile widened. "Scared?"

Tearing open the bag in her lap, she held up a walnut. "Want to swallow this whole for me?"

Don leaned back in his seat, smile trembling at the edges.

"Keep looking at me like that," she said, "and we'll try to do the whole bag, so help me God. Just cram them down there one by one. Trust me, it's two hours in the air, we'll have time."

Don lowered his gaze to the floor. Fiona eased into the cushions and cracked her first nut, chewing down its smoky deliciousness as the plane bounced off the runway. It took every ounce of her self-control to sit there and chew, denying Don even a flicker of fear. The plane felt like it took off vertically, dropping her stomach like an elevator with its cable cut.

After a few minutes, the plane leveled off, and Fiona's stomach crawled to its proper position. Don opened the medical kit and fished out a bottle of pain pills, dry-swallowing three. "That man—the one you, uh, shot—he offered a lot of money," Don said, sniffing. "When you're in a hole, any amount looks good. I'm sorry."

"Is that a tear I see?" Fiona asked.

Don turned his face to the window.

"Usually when people aim a gun at me, I kill them." Fiona bared her teeth. "You're still here, so that's a start. Good thing I remembered you had a plane."

"Said I was *thorry*, damnit, sorry."

"Help me get my boyfriend back, fly me somewhere safe, and we'll call it even, okay?"

Don's lip quavered.

"What?" Fiona asked.

Don shook his head.

Fiona raised her eyebrows. "Don, use your words."

Snot dripped from Don's bruised fruit of a nose. He wiped it on his sleeve, swallowed, and said: "We only paid you half."

"That's right."

"You want to earn the rest? Plus a lot more?"

Fiona cracked another nut, swiping the shell fragments

from her lap onto the carpet. She had never been a fan of littering, but dirtying up a private jet felt downright luxurious.

"Sure," she said.

"Then we go to New York. After Cuba. I know where there's money. A lot of it."

"Why don't you get it yourself?" She had no intention of explaining how New York was permanently off-limits to her and Bill.

"It's in a weird place," he said. "I'd need help. Folks who know how to break into things."

"How much money are we talking?"

He shrugged. "Millions. Enough to solve our debts. And yours."

Fiona stared at the passing clouds, the infinity of cold space beyond the aircraft's thin metal skin. In the window's reflection she glimpsed the pink swirl of Crew Cut's blood disappearing down the drain. That was a righteous kill, she thought. So why did my hands shake? Why did I have such a hard time pulling the trigger?

Maybe a part of you doesn't want to kill anymore.

Maybe, but what choice do I have? This is my life. This is what I do best.

"Tell me more," she said. "But if you're lying to me, God help you." After all the misery he had dumped on her head, it was fun watching Don squirm nervously in his seat.

9

ON THE FAR side of Canal de Entrada, the narrow mouth of the Port of Havana, stands the Castillo De Los Tres Reyes Del Morro, a mouthful of a name for an imposing stone hulk of a fortress. Originally designed to protect the harbor from raids, it now serves as a tourist destination. A few hundred yards further down the shore stands La Cabaña, a crumbling line of fortifications that dates back three centuries; the one and only Che Guevara, hero of the Revolution and eternal T-shirt icon, once used the place for tribunals and executions.

A lot of blood had dripped into the soil here over the years.

Bill hoped not to add to it.

In the decades since Fidel's takeover of the island, La Cabaña had become a museum. The grassy fields behind the stone walls hosted a shining line of antique equipment: wheeled artillery pieces, a MiG jet fighter, and huge missiles still looking ready to deliver the pain to the *Norteamericanos.*

Whenever Bill wanted to clear his head, he liked taking a cab to this side of the harbor, where he would spend hours walking along the fortifications, hoping to hear the answer to his problems on the breeze whispering along the bay. The answers never came, but the view was spectacular.

Speaking of views, the area around La Cabaña offered clear lines of sight and multiple exits. He and Fiona had agreed on this spot a long time ago, in case they were apart when the proverbial cow-patty smacked the fan.

Bill stood near the MiG, smoking a cigar, his duffel bag at his feet. The threatening storm had moved further offshore, leaving the skies clear in time for evening. Above the stone ridge of the fortress, the darkness descended like a slow curtain. Soon the guards would start clearing the park. He hoped Fiona, who had texted him from the airport, would make it in time.

To his right, a narrow road led to Che's House, which the state had converted into a memorial. Bill puffed and worried. Had his new assassin friends seen him leave the hotel? He had taken a cab to Chinatown, where he hailed a second cab to take him across the bay to La Cabaña. Hopefully his spycraft was good enough.

Two figures appeared at the far end of the road, their features hidden by dusk and distance.

Bill dropped the nub of the cigar into the dust, crushed it cold. His fear was a small match burning in his stomach.

The amber sunlight arcing through the trees gleamed on what was unmistakably Fiona's hair, and intense relief snuffed out his fear. She had a canvas duffel bag over her shoulder, her left hand on the strap. Her right hand gripped the shoulder of a thin, gray man Bill had never seen before.

Slinging his bag onto his shoulder, Bill trotted down the road, meeting them halfway. "Excuse me," he said. "I'm a little lost. Can you give me directions?"

Fiona's lips tightened into a bloodless line. "Not the time for jokes, sweetie."

At least she had called him sweetie.

"Sorry," he said, nodding toward the man. "Who's this?"

"Bill, meet Don," Fiona said. "My cigar-factory client? Decided to sell us out to our old friends in the Rockaways."

"Surprised you're still alive," Bill told him, gesturing at his purple nose and bruised cheeks.

Fiona's hand shifted from Don's shoulder to the back of his neck, clenching softly. "He is, too," she said. "But he has something very interesting to tell you, once we get out of here."

Shoving past Don, Bill ran a thumb down Fiona's cheek, notched with faint cuts. "What happened to you out there?"

"Nothing bad," she said, the lie clear in her face.

"Oh, come on." Bill said.

"I'll tell you later. It's a long story." With her free hand, Fiona gripped his thumb and squeezed it twice before letting go. "We got a car down the road a bit. Driver's waiting. Don's plane is at the airport. We can't go direct from the States, because of the whole embargo thing, but

I was thinking we'd go to Mexico City, catch a commercial flight from there."

"Where are we going?" Bill asked.

"New York. Belly of the beast, if you want to get dramatic about it."

"You're kidding."

"Nope." Fiona released Don's neck. "There's a real money-making opportunity, so long as our little buddy here isn't messing with us."

Don's left eye twitched. "Hey, I get well off this, too."

There's no interest like self-interest, Bill thought. "We should move. We're being hunted," he said. "Two hitters."

"Man and a woman?" Fiona asked.

"Yeah."

"Big guy, small lady, real whitebread-looking?"

"Exactly the same, yeah."

"Dressed kinda like tourists?"

"How do you know this?"

Fiona pointed behind him. "Because they're right there."

Bill spun around. No more than thirty feet away, from the direction of La Cabaña, the couple marched toward them in lockstep. The man's hands jammed deep in the pockets of his khakis, the woman's hidden in the folds of her bright skirt. In the fading light, the bottomless depths of their sunglasses made their faces look like skulls.

Pushing up his left sleeve, Bill retrieved the long shard of mirror glass held in place by the strap of his watch, its ragged edges sheathed in a shred of Che T-shirt. The cloth doubled as a handle, so he could clutch the improvised blade in his right hand.

The couple stopped fifteen feet away, close enough for Bill to judge the expensive cuts of the his-and-hers outfits. The man was massive, his neck (partially covered by a loose red kerchief) linebacker-thick, his linen shirt straining against slabs of muscle. Beside him, the woman looked as small and sharp as a bone scalpel.

"Hi, Barbara," Fiona said.

The woman's head tilted slightly. She removed her hands from her pockets and brought them together, knotting her fingers into a ball. Bill noticed her silver watch had a thin band and a chunky face too large for her wrist.

"You know them?" Bill asked.

"Yeah, these bland motherfuckers are Barbara and Ken. Good friends of the Dean," Fiona said, raising her voice. "Right there is fine, thanks."

Ken smiled. "Long time no see, Fiona."

"Believe it or not," Fiona said. "But you're the second guy to say that to me this week. And the first guy's dead, so don't press your luck. We're leaving now."

His shard of glass pressed against his hip, Bill retreated until he stood alongside Fiona, who placed her hand between Don's shoulder-blades. Don seemed in shock, his face pale, his breathing shallow.

Moving in perfect sync, Barbara and Ken stepped forward. It reminded Bill of wolves in nature documentaries, how they worried their prey to death from a distance.

Bill and Fiona retreated, pulling Don by his shirt.

Barbara and Ken mirrored their movement.

Bill heard the low murmur of rubber on gravel. A horn tooted. He risked turning his head. The sight of the white Peugeot, two police officers in the front, dumped a quart of adrenaline into his blood. It took every ounce of his self-composure to keep his feet rooted to the ground.

"This is either really good," Fiona said, "or really, really bad."

The cop car eased to a stop. The police inside took their sweet time climbing out, the one in the passenger seat pausing to adjust his belt before closing the door behind him. Neither appeared too concerned about the situation. They probably assumed everyone here was a tourist.

Fiona offered the cops a wide smile and burbled something in Spanish, too fast for Bill to catch. The cop from the driver's seat smiled and said something back. Barbara and Ken stood still, their hands in their pockets. Bill studied the sidearms in the officers' holsters. How quickly could they draw down on a threat?

The cop from the passenger's side, the one not talking to Fiona, glanced at Bill's waist and startled.

Bill looked down at the shard of glass in his hand.

Oops.

The cop yelled to his partner, his hand darting for his pistol. On reflex, Bill dropped the shard and raised his hands, part of him praying that Fiona had a weapon and could drop these fools, another part hoping they could still talk their way out of this.

The other cop trotted around the front of the Peugeot, his pistol drawn and aimed down. He was clearly following procedure, flanking the group from another angle. It was a smart move, except it brought him too close to Barbara and Ken.

As the cop passed the couple, focused on Bill, his pistol drifting upwards, Barbara's right hand moved over her left wrist. There was a faint click, and the cop swiveled in her direction. Too late. Barbara's hands darted around his head, and a thin line appeared across his throat.

A wire.

She was garroting him with a wire hidden in the watch.

Grunting loud, Barbara rammed a knee into the small of the cop's back, driving him to the ground. A sheet of red ran down his throat and soaked the gray collar of his uniform.

Moving fast for a man of such enormous size, Ken scooped low to retrieve the dying cop's pistol.

The cop's partner fired three times, the bullets zipping over Ken to spark off some priceless Revolutionary hardware. The lead missed Barbara by inches, and yet she seemed as unconcerned as if a few insects had buzzed past her head. She had her left forearm behind the dying cop's head, pressing his face into the gravel as she pulled the wire taut with her right hand. The cop's legs spasmed.

Fiona hurled her duffel underhand at the cop firing his pistol. The bag smashed his elbow as he pulled the trigger a fourth time, sending the bullet on a downward trajectory that, as luck had it, ended at Ken's right wrist.

Ken grunted and dropped his new pistol, his other hand rising to clutch his wound.

Before the cop could turn on her, Fiona sprinted the ten feet between them, her elbow descending on his surprised face. Bill heard the nose break with a loud crunch. The cop gurgled and fell, Fiona wrestling his sidearm from his grip. She had mistimed knocking him cold—if she had waited another half-second, he might have plugged both Ken and Barbara.

"Bill," Fiona said, aiming the pistol at the couple. "Get Don, and get in the cop car. Take the officer, too."

Bill already had a hand on Don's shoulder. "Why?"

"Because they'll kill him if we leave him here."

Ken hooked two fingers into the kerchief around his neck and pulled it loose. Pushing back his red-splattered sleeve, he wrapped the fabric around the wound and cinched it tight. "You know how much this shirt cost?" he asked calmly, unruffled and smooth as a radio announcer reading the weather report.

Barbara unwound her wire from the dead cop's neck and stood, careful to avoid the blood spreading toward her feet. Reaching into the cop's back pocket, she snatched free a handkerchief and used it to clean the dangling wire. The bloodied cloth she let flutter to the ground; pressing a button on the side of the case retracted the wire into the watch.

Bill had seen a lot of dead bodies in his time, some barely recognizable as human thanks to fire or a storm of bullets. He liked to think all that death had driven the squeamishness from him. But watching Ken and Barbara beside the cop's corpse made his skin curdle into gooseflesh.

For years, Bill had regarded Fiona as the epitome of a predator, someone who could pump a bullet into someone's head before heading out to brunch, but even his girlfriend suffered the effects of taking lives. He doubted that Ken and Barbara ever felt anything close to remorse: they treated killing the way someone might sort through bottles of hot sauce at a store.

"Bill," Fiona said. "Get moving."

Bill shoved Don into the backseat of the police car before returning to the unconscious cop on the ground. You had to give Fiona credit: she knew how to use every ounce of her one-hundred-thirty pounds to deliver the hurt to whoever stood in her way. But knocking someone out also turned them into dead weight, and that was a problem for Bill as he strained to load the snoring policeman into the vehicle.

Don squawked, slapping his hands in the air as Bill shoved the cop's body on top of him. Bill smirked back, feeling no amusement whatsoever. None of the numbers looked good: two killers in front of them, maybe a couple minutes at best before someone new appeared on the road.

Tossing their two duffel bags atop the lovebirds in the back, Bill circled to the driver's side. Ducking behind the wheel, he prayed that the cops had left the keys in the ignition.

The ignition was empty.

Bill's heart stopped cold.

When he looked again, a set of shiny keys dangled in the slot.

Oh, brain, you silly joker! Haha!

The vehicle was a stick-shift, and that was okay: Bill's mother had taught him how to work one when he was fifteen. Pressing down the clutch and brake, Bill twisted the key, and the motor coughed awake. How long had it been since he'd last seen a manual gearshift? Twenty years?

Standing outside the car, Fiona flicked her pistol at Ken. "Kick his gun over here."

Ken lashed out with his right foot, sending the dead

cop's gun skittering beneath the Peugeot. He winked at Fiona, daring her to kneel down and look for it. "We're going to kill you," he announced.

"I don't think so," Fiona replied. From the far side of the harbor—maybe closer—drifted a faint siren. She knew she should put this pair down, but it was one against two, and they both moved like devils: blasting one would give the other an opening to attack.

Gritting her teeth, Fiona climbed into the front passenger seat and shut the door, her arm with the pistol poking out the open window. She aimed at the space between Ken and Barbara, making them guess which one she would shoot first if either made a move. "Reverse," she told Bill. "And hit it."

Bill fumbled with the shifter, which lacked one of those little diagrams on top of the knob that traced the gear layout. On his mother's old car, you threw the stick all the way to the right and up in order to engage the reverse. He did that, hoping it was the right choice, and slowly eased up on the clutch while giving the engine a bit of gas.

The engine thumped, choked, and died.

Fiona glanced at him.

"Stick," Bill said, stomping on the clutch and twisting the ignition.

The engine caught on the second try. It was hard to tell over the growl of pistons, but the sirens in the distance had grown louder. Through the windshield, they saw Barbara grin and take a tiny step forward—daring Fiona to pull the trigger.

Bill moved the shifter to the left and up. That was another way to do it, right? On his old car, there was always a deep click as the reverse gear engaged, but he heard nothing. Was he doing it right?

Again he let up on the clutch while pressing down on the gas pedal.

The engine coughed and shuddered silent.

In the backseat, Don moaned in terror.

Bill twisted the key again. "I'll go forward," he said. "They'll get out of the way, dive."

"No," Fiona snapped. "Reverse. Other car's that way."

Barbara turned to Ken and said something. Ken laughed and strolled to his left, toward Bill's side. With every step, he made it harder for Fiona to cover both of them.

The engine grumbled. Bill ran his numb fingers along the shifter, trying to figure out what he might have missed. On the underside of the knob, his thumb skimmed a rubber ring—he lifted it and felt a spring inside the shaft. A distant memory came to him: this was the lift collar, which prevented the driver from accidentally throwing the vehicle into reverse while driving. Sort of like the safety on a gun.

Lifting the collar, he pushed the shifter all the way to the right, and it went further than before. Then he moved it down, just to try something new, and miracle of miracles, that worked, too.

Bill eased the clutch, pushed the gas, and the Peugeot sprang backwards, the motor whining. Their front hood retreated, uncovering the cop's pistol on the gravel. Ken leapt for it, and Fiona opened fire. Puffs of dust exploded around the assassin, forcing him back.

Fiona's pistol snapped open, empty, and she threw it

into the grass alongside the road. Barbara and Ken had disappeared, lost in the puzzle of trees and sunset. In his mirrors Bill could see where the road opened onto an intersection, a black Lada parked on the grassy shoulder. For weeks, Bill had joked with Fiona about those Russian vehicles, four-wheeled death traps with ancient engines. *We get into a wreck in those, we'd be dead*, he said. *They might as well make the seat-belts out of piano wire.* That aside, if that cruddy little car could deliver them to the airport alive, Bill would stoop and kiss its dented bumper out of pure gratitude.

"Thought you knew stick," Fiona said.

"Are we not driving?"

"Whatever."

"Hey, I would have knocked this cop out after he shot them, not before."

"I timed wrong. Shut up."

The cop car bumped onto the shoulder beside the Lada, and Bill stood on the brakes. Before they came to a full stop, Fiona had her door open, a fake smile on her face as she waved at the Lada's driver, who looked nonplussed. He was probably thinking about how ten years in a Cuban jail would go.

Bill shoved Don into the Lada's backseat. Those sirens sounded too close for comfort. At least the knocked-out cop was safe. The inside of the Lada smelled of fried food. Fiona in the front seat told the man to drive, drive, there was a big payment if he delivered them to the airport in record time.

Shoved tight against squirming Don, their duffels under his arm, Bill wondered if he should have shifted the cop car into first gear after all, tried to crush Barbara and Ken like bugs. They won't stop pursuing us, he thought. Not until they're dead, or we are.

10

THE PILOT CLICKED on the intercom to announce they had left Cuban airspace.

Flying in a private jet made Bill's nethers tingle. Despite his love of luxury, he had never risen higher than first class on a domestic flight, where the seats were plush but you often had to share a row with a businessman who loved talking about widget manufacturing protocols. After unclipping his seatbelt, he took a few silent victory laps around the cabin, running his hands over the leather and wood, marveling at the collection of snacks and drinks in the galley.

In her own seat, Fiona clutched the armrests so hard her fingers threatened to punch through the expensive leather. When Bill placed a hand on her shoulder, she brushed it away.

"Jeez," he said. "Sorry."

"You sorry about before?"

He crouched in front of her, close enough to kiss. "I'll spend less."

She leaned forward, her lips brushing past his before arriving at his ear. "You'll listen," she whispered. "That's it. All I want. Got it?"

Bill kissed her on the neck and sprung back, as joyful as a kid freed from detention. Stretching out his arms to touch the gleaming white walls, he sang: *All I want is you.*

Relaxing her grip on the armrests, Fiona grinned. "You want this jet, too."

"You got that right," Bill replied, retrieving a bottle of whiskey from the liquor cabinet, along with three glasses. The elaborate calligraphy on the bottle's label looked Japanese, and the liquid inside smelled top-shelf. "Started from the bottom, now we're here."

"Enjoy it now, because we're in the cheapest possible seats on the way to the States." Fiona turned to Don, who had spent takeoff brooding in a seat at the far end of the cabin. "You want to tell Bill what you told me?"

"First things first," Bill said. "What happened to you in Nicaragua?"

"Remember Crew Cut?" Fiona made fists in case her hands started shaking again. Her arms flared in pain, every nerve a needle in her muscles. Screw aspirin: she needed some of that whiskey. No, actually, a lot of that whiskey.

"He showed up?"

"He did." Unclenching her fists, Fiona nodded at Don. "Because this chump called him."

"And here I was," Bill said, pouring himself a glass of whiskey, "thinking Don was a nice guy."

Fiona laughed. "Can I tell him the landmine story?"

Don sighed, his head drooping. "Whatever."

"The first time I go down to Nicaragua," Fiona said, "I drive over to the tobacco fields that supply these guys' factory. And I see this ratty pickup filled with a bunch of drunk guys, driving back and forth over every square inch of the field. Don and his idiot brother are standing on this little hill, watching them do it.

"I park my car and ask them what's going on, and Don said: 'We paid these guys at the bar five bucks apiece to drive around our new field, look for landmines.' Can you believe it? Potentially ending three guys' lives, just because they're too cheap to hire a professional to actually clear mines. How much does your cigar label earn per year, Don? Must be in the millions, right? Why the hell do you even have cash problems?"

"Hey," Don said. "Those guys in the field? They took the money. Free markets."

Fiona grunted. "So I pull out my pistol and fire it in the air until those guys stop driving. Don gets a little peeved over it. His brother's too busy staring at my ass. Anyway, Don phoned up Crew Cut, who is very dead."

Bill waved his glass at Don's wrecked face. "Looks like you got some payback."

"Nah, that wasn't payback," Fiona said. "True payback would be shooting Don in the head and leaving him in a ditch. But he came up with a business opportunity."

"Enough money to buy this plane?" Bill asked.

"Because I'm digging this mode of travel. I don't think I can go back to commercial flights, honey, I'm sorry."

"My father owned a bar near Union Square," Don said. "He was a World War II vet, made a lot of money."

"Which bar?" Bill asked, after downing his glass and refilling it. Damn good whiskey. He topped off the other two, handing the slightly fuller one to Fiona before walking the other across the cabin to Don.

"Dusty's. Our old man's last name was Dyzek, but he changed it to Dusty before we were born. I don't know why he chose that name."

"You never asked?"

"Dad's motto is punch first, answer questions later." As much as Don tried to make his shrug look casual, Bill could read the pain in his face. "Anyway, he gave his new name to the bar, too. His father—my grandfather—started the place, but I don't think it really had a name at the start. They probably called it 'The Tavern' or some shit."

Bill handed him the glass. "I think I went there a few times. Looked like nobody had cleaned it in fifty years, right? Cheap drinks, though."

"It wasn't dirty, it was authentic," Don said. "We sold it ten years ago. The rent was too damn high. It's an art gallery now. Story of everything in Manhattan. The cool stuff goes away, gets replaced by overpriced crap."

"This is the part where you tell me what your family's bar has to do with anything," Bill said, bringing his glass to his lips. Empty. That was odd. He had no memory of draining it. He fetched the bottle from the far side of the cabin, ignoring the voice in his head that told him to take it easy on the drinking.

"There's gold under the floorboards. It used to be in a box," Don said. "Dad's the paranoid type, so he bought this enormous safe. It could probably take a nuclear blast and stay shut."

"How did it get there?" Fiona asked. The whiskey warmed her body, driving back the pain. A little.

Don mimed firing a rifle. "Dad found it in Europe, during the War. Never told us where or how. Just in case you haven't picked up on it yet, he isn't exactly the warm and fuzzy type."

"He's still alive?" Bill freshened his whiskey.

"Oh yeah," Don said. "Ninety-two years old and still a bastard. I'm convinced the old man's invincible. Nothing's been able to kill him so far: not cancer, not a couple of heart operations, not falling off his roof when he was fixing it."

Fiona made a speed-it-up motion with her finger. "Why didn't you take the gold when you sold the place?"

"Um, we didn't know it was there." Don spoke slowly, as if explaining something to a child. "Dad never mentioned it. Probably afraid we'd try to steal it. We sold the bar long-distance, from Managua, and when I called him about it, he starts yelling that I'm an idiot, that we lost a whole fortune."

"That's what you get for selling it from underneath your old man," Bill said. "And let me guess: you didn't mention it to the gallery owners or anyone, because you were scared someone else would try and take it from you."

"Yeah. And we were too busy with the cigar business."

Don squirmed. "Every week, I search online, looking for articles about someone digging up a ton of gold in an art gallery. Nothing. I guess the current owners didn't rip up the floor."

"And you never tried stealing it before now?" Fiona asked. Don smirked. "Never met any thieves."

"Careful," Bill said, waving the bottle, "or you're not getting a refill."

"I'm sorry," Don said, holding out his glass. "I owe Fiona. I'm sorry for what I did. But that's not the only reason. I want a big cut. It's my family's gold."

Erupting in the fakest laughter this side of a used-car dealership, Bill walked over and poured a single amber drop into Don's glass. "How much?"

"Thirty percent," Don said, shaking his glass.

Bill poured another lonely drop. "That's a little rich. Ten percent."

"Twenty percent."

Bill poured a bigger splash of whiskey. "Twelve."

Fiona rolled her eyes. "It might be twelve percent of nothing. Your father wouldn't be the first dude to blow smoke up everybody's asses over how much money he had."

"Dad's not the lying type," Don said. "He's got the key, at his house in Queens. Unless you want to try and hack the safe, or blow it up, whatever, I suggest we head over there when we land. And I'm warning you now: he might look old, but he's vicious as hell."

PART THREE

OUT OF THE PAST

1

NEW YORK, NEW YORK: big city of dreams, the closest thing Bill and Fiona had to a hometown. This shiny marvel of glass and steel, much of its old grit washed away by an endless flood of money, the flop houses and junkie haunts of the Village transformed into condos with doormen and gyms, the dank bars replaced by all-organic eateries, the grimy old buried deep below the ultra-expensive new. If you wanted the underbelly, you needed to dig for it.

Bill, much to his regret, had arrived in New York too late to experience the Bad Old Days, when you could stand on a corner in Times Square and quickly field offers for any number of goods and services, from cheap pistols to a pipe loaded with premium crack. Stand in the same place today, and you would most likely draw someone dressed as a superhero or oversized cartoon, squeaking and stunting for a crisp dollar. In those first days of his long residency, Bill found himself tempted to pickpocket tourists, if only to inject some of the old spirit back into the city. The scattering of police cameras on every corner always made him think better of it.

Nor would he have much opportunity to cause mischief on this trip: Fiona had him on the tightest of leashes, especially after he told her about abandoning most of her stuff in Havana. From the airport in Newark they had taken a cab to the nearest train station, paid cash for tickets, and crossed under the Hudson on a local. Rising from the maze of train tracks and concrete platforms into the dingy bustle of Penn Station, Bill's pulse accelerated to maniac tempo. This city he loved so much would become a death-trap if they made a single wrong move.

Standing beside him on the escalator, Fiona spied the single drop of sweat trickling down Bill's forehead and prayed that he would keep his cool long enough to complete this mission. Sure, Bill had already survived quite a bit, and yes, he came with his own set of street smarts—but just as metal in a forge begins to warp and bend when you apply too much heat, the past few months had made him more brittle at the edges.

"Where are we going first?" Don asked them.

"Queens," Fiona said. "Taking the subway."

"I haven't called my Dad." Don's nose was healing nicely: aside from the occasional slurred syllable, he sounded almost normal. "He has no idea we're coming, and he really doesn't like surprises."

"We'll deal with it," Bill said. "How bad can he be?"

"You'll see," Don snapped back. "He can kick your ass."

"I'd buy a ticket to that," Fiona muttered.

Bill smirked and adjusted the wrists of his dark blue hoodie. Fiona and Don wore the same sweatshirts, purchased in a seedy kiosk in Jersey. The screaming eagles on their chests made them look like ultra-patriotic monks. It sucked as a disguise, but the hoods might prevent anyone in the station from getting too good a look at their faces. Bill and Fiona knew the Dean had a few men lurking around Midtown.

The bags over their shoulders held clothes and Fiona's cash and not much else. When Fiona thought about gold, she pictured enormous piles of gleaming coins, like something out of a pirate fantasy. It was enough to propel her aching, bruised body down the ramp to the subway. If we survive this, she told herself, we're going to spend some of that treasure on a five-star hotel room. And once we settle in, I'm going to fill the tub with ice and soak in it for a month. I'll prevent hypothermia by hooking my veins to an IV bag full of top-shelf vodka. I deserve nothing less.

The subway rumbled them across Manhattan and the East River in twenty minutes, the tracks rising into Long Island City, its skyline jagged with new high-rises. Bill held a palm to his mouth, stifling a yawn: the overnight flight from Mexico City to Jersey, crammed in steerage with dozens of sunburned tourists, had left him feeling drained as a vampire's victim. At least customs had swept them through without so much as a second glance, despite their bruises and last-minute plane tickets.

They left the train at the Court Square station and

walked down the iron stairway to the street, lined on either side with elegant brownstones and tall, arching trees. The street was empty except for a couple of teenagers on the corner, staring at a video on a phone.

"Swanky neighborhood," Bill said, nodding appreciatively. "You know, for all the time I lived in New York, I don't think I ever made it to Long Island City. No, wait, isn't there that restaurant…"

"M. Wells," Fiona said. "Couple blocks north."

"Waffles with caviar on them." Bill smiled. "Good cocktails. Your Dad must have done well for himself, Don."

Don shook his head. "My father bought his place when it was a normal neighborhood. We weren't special. But he held on all this time, God bless him, so I guess that makes him a millionaire on paper."

The brownstones stood three stories tall, fronted with elegantly curved windows and doors. They walked midway down the block, stopping in front of a house that stood out like a dead tooth in a row of pearly whites: the windows soaped with dirt and covered with cardboard, the stoop crumbling, the gutters crumpled. A sun-faded sign tacked to the front door announced: 'COME BACK WITH A WARRANT.'

"If this neighborhood ever had, you know, one of those contests for the best-looking house?" Bill said. "This house would lose every single time."

Don sighed. "My father sort of stopped giving a shit." Fiona squinted at the sign. "He hasn't lost his sense of humor, though."

"No, he's serious," Don said. "I heard he gets noise

complaints all the time. I keep in touch with the neigh-bors, just in case anything happens. Can we get this over with?"

Don climbed the stairs first, followed by Bill, then Fiona with her hands in her pockets. When they reached the top, Don took a deep breath, held it, and knocked on the door. No response. He pressed an ear to the rough wood and shook his head. "Don't hear anything," he said.

Bill gripped the brass knob and twisted hard. "Maybe it's unlocked…"

Don raised a hand. "Don't—"

A small hole appeared in the door to the left of Bill's head, accompanied by a muffled thump. Bill stumbled backward, swiping at flecks of wood and paint in his eyes, and almost tumbled over the railing before Fiona grabbed his collar and yanked him toward her. Their dropped bags flopped down the steps. All three crouched as two more holes popped beside the first, raining blue and green paint-chips on the stone.

"Dad," Don called. "Dad, stop!"

From the other side of the door, they heard a voice rough as ball bearings in a blender. "Son, is that you?"

"Yes," Don smiled. "Yes, it's me."

Another hole punched through the wood, the bullet missing Don by an inch as he landed facedown on the stoop. "I get you, you little prick?" asked the voice.

"Yeah, he's dead," Fiona called, winking at Don.

A long pause. "Who are you?"

"His probation officer," Fiona said. "He was coming to say how sorry he was."

"Yeah, he's sorry now," the voice retorted. "I'm sorry

for the shooting, but you know my sons left me to die in here? Those ungrateful bastards."

"I'm sorry, sir," Fiona said, easing upright as quietly as she could. "I'm not police. Can you open the door so we can talk about this?"

"Say you're not police."

"I'm not police." Fiona glanced across the street, curious if the bullets had smashed any windows. No faces visible, no screams or sirens. God bless a neighborhood where everyone had an office job during the day.

"Say it again," the voice asked.

Bill twirled a finger beside his temple.

"I'm not police," Fiona said, gesturing for Bill to move back from the door.

A heavy bolt thumped, and the door cracked open. Fiona raised her foot and drove it into the metal plate beneath the knob, snapping the door wide. In the shadowy foyer sat an ancient man in a wheelchair, a thick red blanket draped over his legs. He wore a threadbare gray T-shirt that displayed his wrinkled biceps. In his left hand he held a small silver pistol.

Before he could pull the trigger again, Fiona darted forward and nipped the scorching-hot weapon from his gnarled fingers. "Trespassing," he said, leveling his faded blue eyes at cowering Don and Bill.

"That cop thing is bullshit, by the way," Fiona said, moving past him to check the hallway beyond. "Undercover cops, they don't have to tell you the truth if you ask three times. Figured you'd know that, since you're older than dirt." Rows of cardboard boxes lined the wall to her right. To her left, a pair of glass doors opened onto a darkened living room. She tossed the pistol atop the highest stack of boxes, well out of reach of someone in a wheelchair.

"My name's James Dusty," the man said. "I apologize for my weak sons. I can't explain it, my sperm is strong."

"Thanks, Dad," Don said, grimacing as he stood and dusted himself off. Beside him, Bill unzipped his hoodie, offering a lovely view of his sweat-stained shirt beneath.

"I'm Fiona," she said. "That sweaty guy is Bill, my boy-friend. We're very pleased to meet you. We have a lot to discuss."

"You got a fine ass," James said, wheeling his chair down the hallway after her. "Maybe we could talk about that."

He is a senior citizen, a voice in her head reminded her. Do not inflict pain upon an old guy, even if he did try to shoot you. He's a veteran, like your father.

Screw it, I've had too long a week to act nice.

"I'd grab your cock and rip it off," she said, spinning on him, "but I didn't bring any tweezers. So why don't you cut the shit and tell me about the gold?"

2

THE KITCHEN STANK of burnt beans and grease. James ground his wheels over the stacks of takeout menus, used styrofoam cartons, and newspapers that covered the scratched linoleum. He parked himself at the round table at the far end of the room, and gestured for the rest of them to sit. Fiona evaluated the chairs piled high with mail and opted to lean against the ancient sink. Bill, always mindful of stains, placed their bags in the hall and stood in the kitchen doorway, careful not to touch anything.

Don ignored the mess. Clearing a chair of junk, he plopped down, exhaling loudly. "Like what you've done with the place," he told his father.

"You're talking pretty brave for someone I almost plugged," James said. "You wet yourself when that bullet shot past, boy?"

Don gestured toward his pants. "Dry as a bone. Do better next time."

"Gentlemen," Fiona said. "If we could stop the pissing match for just a moment, I'll break down the situation for you, because I don't think we have a lot of time. James, the bar you used to own, it has gold underneath the floor, right?"

"This dimwit tell you everything?" James asked, baring his yellow teeth at his son. "He had the balls—the absolute balls—to call up and say he'd sold it because he needed the money for his precious cigar factory. That place was mine, you little shit. I kept it running, just so you and your tubby-ass brother could take it from me."

"You hadn't been there in a decade," Don said, his jaw tight.

"I love family harmony," Bill said, edging away from the wall as a massive cockroach scuttled past. "Reminds me so much of my own home growing up."

Fiona shot him a look: cool it.

"What's your interest?" James asked Fiona.

"Your son almost got me killed. He offered me a cut of the gold as a make-good," Fiona said. "I took him up on it."

"He offered it to you?" The old man laughed until he began to cough, his thin frame shuddering. When he recovered, he cleared his throat and rasped: "He offered it? That gold is mine."

"Maybe you can spend it on a cleaning lady," Don said, kicking at a pile of yellowed tabloids near his foot.

"We can negotiate," Fiona said. "I'm open."

"It's my gold," James said. "All of it. I earned it back when my last name was Dyzek."

"And you're not getting an ounce unless someone digs it up," Fiona said. "Think it over."

James turned his head to the window, as if the rusty fridge and thick weeds in the yard could give him insight into this conundrum. "Fine," he said. "Eighty-twenty."

Fiona laughed. "Your son wanted a cut, too."

Don nodded furiously. "Fifteen percent."

"You're not dealing with this little pissant," James said, thumping a fist lightly against the side of his wheelchair. "You're dealing with me. I scalped and shot a lot of Nazi bastards for that gold, which entitles me to eighty fucking percent. And if you have a problem with that, I will get out of this wheelchair, so help me God, and boot your fine head through that fucking wall. I don't care that you're a woman."

Fiona laughed and turned to Bill. "I like him."

Bill shrugged. Standing in this hoarder's abode, with its weird smells and tight spaces, made him nervous. He wanted out of here. Sooner or later—probably on the sooner side, knowing his luck this week—word would trickle back to the Rockaway Mob that its favorite fugitives had returned to the Big Apple, and a lot of scary people would pour onto the streets after them.

Fiona swiveled back to James. "Fifty-fifty, because we have to go dig it up. And like I said, there's no digging it up without us. I checked online when we were coming here, the gallery's closed today. We go in this evening, it gives us a lot of hours to work the problem."

James shrugged. "Not like I can spend that much

money in the time I got left," he said. "Probably can't get laid without my ticker blowing up. So, sure, fifty percent."

Fiona clapped her hands. "That safe got a key or a combination?"

James nodded at the sideboard, where a small ceramic bowl sat precariously on a tower of past-due notices. "Key's in there," he said. "On the keychain. The old-looking one with the wolf's head."

Fiona found it. "You have my word on fifty percent," she said.

"We'll see," James said. "You're just some chick who bangs in here, says everything's all good." He jutted his chin at Bill. "Your boy-toy here stays behind, until you come back."

No can do," Bill said. "I'm the one who knows locks."

"Then the woman stays," James said. "I don't give a crap. I wasn't born yesterday, sonny. How much of an idiot do you have to be to call yourself an expert in turning a key?"

"Don't answer that," Fiona said, tossing a wink in Bill's direction. "Okay, we have an agreement. But if anything happens to him while I'm gone, all deals are off, okay?"

"Don't I get a say?" Bill asked, spinning to survey the mountains of trash, the scurrying critters, the sink piled with plates and scorched pans. "Every minute I stay here, I feel like my risk of catching Ebola goes up."

"Aw, it's okay," Fiona said. "His gun's on those boxes in the hallway, if you get nervous."

"How are you going to carry all that gold?" Don asked. "Or break through the floor?"

James shrugged. "Listen, girl, my boy here is the

biggest idiot alive, but he still got a point. When I bought the safe, I buried it in the northeast corner of the room… you can tell directions, right?"

"Don't try me," Fiona snapped.

James held up his hands in mock surrender. "Apologies. Go to the northeast corner. It's ten feet along the north wall, ten feet south. Break through the floorboards, it should be right there. Got no idea why they haven't found that gold yet. My guess is they never tried putting in new flooring when they made their pussy little gallery. Got that?"

"Distressed flooring is in," Bill said. The idea of spending a few hours in this house did not sit well with him, pistol or no.

"Don't you fret," Fiona said. "I have this criminal thing down cold." On her way out the doorway, she slipped a hand into Bill's hip pocket, giving his thigh a friendly squeeze before extracting the phone he brought from Cuba. "I'm going to borrow this."

"Stay safe," he said, touching her wrist.

"You watch yourself," she replied.

"Is that a request, or a threat?"

"Bit of both." Fiona smiled and turned for the door.

The next time she saw Bill, his face would be nearly as battered as hers.

3

FIONA SENT A few texts from Bill's phone as the subway carried her one stop to Queensboro Plaza. When she was a kid, this area had been little more than a grime-smeared ramp to the Queensboro Bridge, lined with strip clubs and fast-food joints and an Army recruitment center. Now it hosted the corporate headquarters of a major airline, a youth hostel gleaming with blue lights, and a row of restaurants that charged thirty bucks for a burrito or a burger.

But the grit was still there, if you knew where to look.

Walking up a quiet side-street that angled away from the Plaza was like rewinding a couple decades back in time. She passed boarded-up storefronts, a small bodega with a torn awning, an empty lot piled high with wet gravel and shredded tires. A sign on the lot's chain-link fence proclaimed this block was the future site of Scion Condominiums, "A Wonderful Place to Live!"

At the end of this throwback street squatted a concrete warehouse, windowless and unmarked. Fiona slipped through a gap in the fence that separated the loading dock from the street, waving at a pleasant-looking boy in a black wool suit who emerged silently from the building's shadow.

The boy escorted her inside, down a narrow corridor lit by a line of bare bulbs. They crammed into an ancient elevator with an accordion door, which groaned and wheezed its way up five floors.

The car stopped with a disconcerting thump, and they entered another infinite hallway. The boy led her to a steel door, this one blackened by fire. Fiona took a deep breath, smelling incense and fried chicken.

The boy knocked, the door booming loud under his knuckles.

"Come," said a voice from inside.

They entered a lifesize jewel-box, every inch a study in elegance. Thick Persian rugs covered the floors, and the walls gleamed with mirrors and daguerreotypes in ornate frames. Thick velvet drapes covered the windows. At the far end of the space, behind an enormous wooden desk, sat a figure who looked more wolf than man: his gray sideburns thick and tangled, his nose a narrow ramp supporting a pair of round sunglasses with gold rims. This was Simon Genka, a man with his fingers in a little bit of everything.

Back when Fiona did dirty deeds for the Rockaway Mob and the Dean, Simon had ensured she had the best tools, albeit for a premium price. Like many people raised in the world's roughest backwaters, Simon had a taste for expensive fabrics and timepieces, something that Fiona also recognized in Bill.

"It's been a long time," Simon said, gesturing to a baroque chair with gold armrests on the far side of the desk. "I won't ask how you're doing. Only idiots ask that question. I can tell by your face. Ouch. What can I do for you?"

If you believed the stories, Simon had once drunk the blood of a dead rival out of the man's leather boot. You could dismiss half the tales you heard on the street, but the stoniness of Simon's eyes always made Fiona believe that one. Good thing he nearly always wore sunglasses; the smoked lenses made it a little easier to talk to him.

"Equipment," Fiona said.

"For protection?" Simon leaned over the silver tray on his left, where a teapot steamed alongside two cups and ceramic bowls filled with sugar cubes. "Child, with all due apologies, because I know you're a tough lady, but a pistol isn't enough for you. Not now, not with your kind of enemies. I can, however, make arrangements for your safety. For a price."

"A pistol will actually do me a lot of good," Fiona said, holding up the fingers for two sugars while Simon poured tea. "Plus something a little heavier."

Simon passed her a cup. "Taking the war to some old friends?"

"No. Different show. One night only. Then I'm back out." Simon nodded. "Then I am at your service."

"I appreciate it." She took a sip of the sweet brew, letting the silence stretch out before asking: "You hear anything from the Dean?"

"He's still angry, of course." Simon's lips jerked an inch or two: his version of a smile. "In the past few months, he's probably earned several times over what your boyfriend stole from him. Doesn't matter. With a man like that, it's always the principle. You want a meet? See if he'll listen to reason?"

"No." Fiona's teacup trembled slightly in her hand. "Just hoping to avoid him until our work is complete."

Simon cocked his head. "I was joking about a meet."

"I'm running on zero sleep. Makes me sensitive."

"I see. Your hand is shaking. That's unlike you."

She clenched her hand until the trembling stopped. "Comes with the territory."

Simon shrugged. "This work, your special one-night appearance, as you call it: there's money involved, I assume?"

"You assume correct."

"Then I want a cut, when you return the equipment. Consider it a finder's fee."

I hope there's a metric shit-ton of gold under those floorboards, Fiona thought. Otherwise once everyone takes their slice, we're leaving New York with a grand total of twenty bucks. But what choice do I have? "Sure thing," she said. "And one other item, on top of everything else: I'll need a van, clean as possible. It'll get returned, no damage. You still doing vehicles?"

Simon raised a hand, snapped his fingers. The well-dressed boy slipped into view beside the desk. "He'll sort you out," Simon said. "However your score turns out, my compensation will be generous, understand? Tell Ivan what you need."

After Fiona recited her list, and the boy returned to the shadows, she took another sip of tea and settled back. From the inner pocket of his pinstripe jacket, Simon extracted a pack of cigarettes and held it up. Fiona shook her head, noting the Chinese script on the label. Simon, one of the richest men she knew, smoked the same cheap brand he used to buy as a small-time hustler in Flushing.

"Have we reached the psychoanalysis portion of our program?" she asked. The only thing Simon loved more than selling goods to criminals was picking at their brains, as curious as a watchmaker with a new timepiece.

Simon tugged free a coffin-nail with his teeth and lit it with a gold lighter. Taking a few puffs, he leaned back and studied the smoke-ghosts rolling into the dimness above. "Criminals are stupid," he said.

"Tell me about it."

"Real morons. That's why they commit crimes. It's not like they can hold down a real job."

"Preaching to the choir, buddy."

"That's why you fascinate me," Simon said, blasting smoke through his nostrils like a dragon. "Not in a sexual way, of course. But you're bright. You could've done anything else, gone legit, made a fortune."

"I hate cubicles," Fiona said.

"Good a reason as any." Simon squinted through the carcinogen haze. "You haven't killed Bill yet?"

"Nope. Although he's been pissing me off lately."

"I don't blame you. What Bill did was insane, stealing money from the Dean like that." Simon's eyebrows arched.

"I was surprised when you backed his play instead of putting a bullet in his head."

Fiona shrugged.

"When I was your age, I hated it when older men tried offering me advice. So I feel a little odd doing the same to you, but here it goes: no matter how much you love Bill, no matter how much you think he loves you, you'll need to get rid of him sooner or later." Simon raised a hand in the air, as if anticipating her protests. "I know what you're going to say: love conquers all. And it might, for normal people. But we are not normal people. Rain dogs like us, we worship one God, and that's survival."

"What the hell is a rain dog?"

"Term from an old album. It means the criminals, the down-and-outers…"

"I get it. I wasn't going to say love conquers all."

Simon blew a smoke-ring. "Of course, that would have been boring."

"I was going to say: John Wayne and Jimmy Stewart."

"Two great actors."

"Guess which one was the war hero in real life."

Simon thought about it. "John Wayne."

"Why?"

"Because he was John Wayne."

"You're wrong."

"Jimmy Stewart? No, he was a weakling. A sap."

"*Au contraire, mon frere.* He was the highest-ranked actor in the U.S. military, ever. Flew combat missions over Germany, bombed a couple of U-boat docks, delivered the pain." Fiona's hand imitated a bomber flying through the air. "Not only that, he volunteered for it. He figured that, because his granddaddies were in the Civil War, and his daddy fought in World War I, that meant he needed to do his duty, Hollywood star or no."

"How do you know so much about this?"

"When I got shot—the second time—I spent four weeks in bed. Watched a lot of documentaries. Anyway, you know what John Wayne did during World War II?"

"Nothing?"

"You guessed right. John Wayne stayed home. Blamed it on the studio not wanting to lose one of their biggest stars. Toured some bases and hospitals, but he didn't exactly fight to get to the front."

"That's sad." Simon shook his head slowly. "John Wayne was a huge patriot."

"Sure, later in life. Maybe out of guilt, if you want to play armchair psychiatrist."

Simon took a final puff of his cigarette and stubbed it out in the ashtray beside his elbow. "What's this got to do with Bill?"

"Bill is Jimmy Stewart. He doesn't look like much, and he's a little too obsessed with fashion and luxury and all that crap, but he's a survivor." It was Fiona's turn to smile. "The way he dresses, it's like a suit of armor against the world. His way of keeping the mess, the chaos back. You know what that's like."

"He's still not much of a fighter."

"No, he's not. But if that was any sort of qualification, there are a dozen guys I'd have married by now. There's more to life than fighting. Bill gets that. He's the one who keeps me from getting too blood-simple."

Simon's face glowed red as he lit a fresh cigarette. "You know the Dean's sent people after you."

"I know," Fiona said. "Barbara and Ken, can you believe it? We ran into them in Havana yesterday."

"I'm surprised you're still alive."

"Cops showed up."

"Then you were lucky. I met them once, when I was in the market for good freelancers. Remember what I usually ask killers?"

"Why they do it?"

"Yes. Barbara looks at me like I'm stupid and says, 'The money.' I just looked at her, and she added, 'I need a new pair of boobs.' Ken volunteered that he wanted a new Porsche and a time-share. Most criminals, even if they really have no morals, they like to pretend that they do."

"Not those two."

"No. They're creatures of pure desire. No morals, no ethics, no mercy. Amazing that they found each other. Reminds me of you and Bill, actually."

Fiona chuckled. "Screw you, Simon."

"No, no, not the 'no morals' part." Simon bowed his head, letting the confusion pass, before resuming: "People like Ken and Barbara, they're meant to be lone wolves, and yet they found each other somehow. That's how they're like you and Bill."

"That's very romantic of you, Simon. You sure you're not softening in your old age?"

"Never."

Fiona set down her tea. "I shot a man in Oklahoma."

"Correction: you shot several men in Oklahoma."

"You know the one I mean. That assassin the Dean

sent. The crazy one. Only he wasn't attacking me, he was trying to help." She felt a tingling in her hands, like a live wire beneath the flesh. "It bothers me."

"Don't be so hard on yourself," Simon said. "With the crazy ones, who knows what they'll do. You can't take chances."

The voltage in her hands increased, the muscles beginning to twitch. "I shot someone else, yesterday, but I almost couldn't."

"That guilt, I've always called that the Slaughterhouse Blues. Gets us all, sometimes. I used to have nightmares, back when I still slept."

"I can't imagine you sleeping."

"Never for long, or deeply. Ken and Barbara, they don't get the Slaughterhouse Blues. Remember that if you see them again. It might stop your hands from shaking."

"Aw, you care."

Blasting smoke out his nose, Simon shook his head. "Child, I just want my cut. You bring me back something good, you hear? I have expenses."

As Fiona stood to leave, Simon rose from his chair and executed a neat little bow. She had a better view of his jacket, and what she had assumed was pinstriping. In place of solid stripes, the tailor had sewn lines of a succinct phrase in tiny type: FUCK YOU. You can take the hustler off the street, but you can't take the street out of the hustler.

4

AFTER FIONA LEFT, Bill retrieved the pistol from atop the boxes in the hallway and returned to the kitchen, where he leaned against the cleanest-looking wall. No way in hell will I open that fridge, he thought. No matter how hungry I am. The fungus inside has probably built a complex civilization, complete with nuclear weapons.

James squinted at Bill. "Gimme my gun," he said.

Bill shook his head.

James gripped the handles of his wheelchair. "Don't fuck with me, son. I will come over there and take it from you."

"Not if I tip a chair in your way."

"C'mon, Dad," Don said. "Just chill."

"When my father was sick, I took care of him." James jabbed a gnarled finger at his son. "To the bitter fucking end, no matter how much it cost me. It was the least I could do. I'm sorry I raised a piece of shit who couldn't do the same. Where's your brother?"

Don took a deep breath, held it, exhaled loudly. "Nicaragua."

"Is he still a fat fuck?"

Bill's stomach growled. "Speaking of fat," he said, "I want takeout. Anyone want in on that?"

"Good Chinese place a couple blocks away," James said, nodding at the phone attached to the wall near Bill's head. "Number's written there."

"Should you be eating that?" Don asked. "Too much sodium?"

"During the War, we had C-rations," James said. "It tasted like cold rat assholes. Don't tell me what I can put in my body. I'm your fucking father."

With a theatrical shrug, Bill picked up the cracked handset and dialed the digits scrawled in faint pencil on the paint beside it. The voice that answered, over a cacophonous din of crashing pots, told him it would take ten minutes to deliver an order of sesame chicken and some wonton, okay? Yes, that was very okay. Fat and salt was exactly what the doctor ordered.

Hanging up, Bill turned to James, who had steepled his hands beneath his chin, looking almost professorial as he studied his son. Don fixated on the table as if the world's most fascinating object had suddenly appeared there.

"Where'd you find that gold, anyway?" Bill asked.

"Told you, during the War," said James, ever the conversationalist.

"I picked up on that part," Bill smirked. "But what

actually happened? We got nothing going on right now, man. You might as well tell me a good story."

James cleared a gallon of phlegm from his throat. "My unit was in Germany," he said. "We raided a house occupied by a group of Nazi officers. Bad men, the kind who had overseen the camps. Upstairs we found some bags filled with gold teeth, gold coins, bits of jewelry. I remember how heavy those bags were. My memory's been going the past couple years, but what sticks with me is how much muscle it took to drag all of it down the stairs."

Bill shivered. "You brought the teeth back?"

James chuckled. "And not just those from the house. Yanked a few out of some German mouths. My family's Polish, it was payback. My buddies who worked supply, they snuck the loads back into the States. We melted everything down. You know how much they paid us in the Army? Nothing. That gold was fair salary for getting my ass shot at."

"Why not bury it here?" The backyard looked plenty soft for digging, once you cleared away the heaps of mushy cardboard and the rusty hulks of refrigerators past. Plus the tall brick walls blocked any snooping neighbors.

"Always felt funny about having it too close, like someone might try to rob me. And I really did think we'd always own the bar," James said, glaring evil at Don. "Guess I was wrong on that front, thanks to this pissant over here."

Don tapped the table. "What happened to those officers?"

"The ones we took the gold from?" James snarled. "We dragged them outside and shot them all in the backs of their blonde Nazi heads, pop-pop-pop. I know I've done a lot of bad in my life, but I can go to my grave knowing I did that little bit of good."

There was a knock on the front door.

"Food's here," Don said, standing up.

Bill glanced at the clock on the wall. "Bit too early, huh?"

"Like my Dad said, the restaurant's close." Shoving past Bill, Don walked into the hallway. "I know I didn't ask for anything, but you better believe I'm going to steal a bit of whatever you ordered."

Bill flexed his grip on the pistol. His palms suddenly wet. "Hold up, man."

James sensed Bill's tone. His wrinkled hands slipped beneath the thick red blanket covering his legs.

Don was halfway down the hallway, one hand fishing in his jeans pocket for his wallet, when the front door slammed inward. Ken stood in the doorway, so tall he blocked the sun.

What happened next, Bill had to admit, was impressive. Despite his busted leg, Don dove to his right with the panicked speed of a rabbit on quality meth, crashing through the glass doors that separated the hallway from the living room. Through the wall, Bill heard Don's body thumping and crashing over boxes and furniture.

Ken locked on Bill. Whereas in Havana the assassin had rocked tropical-appropriate khakis and a straw hat, now he opted for hitman chic: a black suit with a dark gray shirt and a black tie. It made him look like a used-car salesman who lifted weights on the weekends. There's nothing worse than a serial killer with poor taste and a credit card.

Bill raised the pistol and squeezed the trigger, Ken in

his gunsight ducking outside, disappearing behind the doorframe. Bill's shot rocketed down the hallway and across the street, sparking off the brownstone opposite.

"What's happening?" James yelled.

"Bad people," Bill said, retreating into the kitchen. The pistol threatened to slip from his sweaty fingers. His breath too fast and tight.

"Got one in the yard, too," James said.

Time to get your shit together. Bill glanced over his shoulder in time to see, through the dirty window, a dim white shape drop over the brick wall. "Her name is Barbara. She's a killer," Bill said, attention shifting to the silver .22 automatic in the old man's lap. "Wait, where the hell did you get that?"

"Your girlie-girl wasn't going to reach in my pants," James cackled. "Perfect place to hold a weapon. She couldn't handle *these* goods."

A thump from the hallway. Bill took a deep breath, grit his jaw, and swiveled, catching a black flicker as Ken disappeared through the splintered doors to the living room. Too late to shoot. A window shattered, followed by rapid footsteps, and Don wobbled into view on the stoop, shaking bits of glass and wood out of his hair.

Bill gestured for Don to come down the hallway. Don flashed him the finger and disappeared down the stairs to the street.

So much for family loyalty.

Bill knew the dining room behind him was piled high with crap, and that a tall bookshelf and several crushed boxes barricaded the door at its far end. That door had two dead-bolts. If it led outside, all that weight and steel might prevent Barbara from entering, unless she scaled to the second floor. Who knew what crazy acrobatic skills she had?

Better to handle Ken first, then deal with his nutso girlfriend.

"Old-timer," Ken's voice drifted from the living room. "You got a gun?"

"I do," James called out. "Locked and loaded."

"Then how about you aim it at Bill there, and let us take him off your hands."

James cocked his head. "And you'll let me live?"

Bill offered him a look that said: Really, man? Really? "Yes. It's okay, you don't really have a choice," Ken said. "You're surrounded."

From the dining room came the faint creak of a doorknob twisting, the thump of wood straining against a lock.

"We got gold," James said.

Sweat trickled down the back of Bill's neck. If I fire through the walls and run, he thought, can I keep Ken's head down long enough to make the door? Your chances are roughly one in three million. You're basically dealing with the Terminator, remember.

"So you've got gold." Ken said. "Ever think of spending it on a little upkeep?"

"It's from teeth," James said, as if that explained everything. A long silence from Ken, followed by: "Huh?"

Screw it, I'm not going to die listening to this crap. Bill leveled the pistol and tried to pinpoint Ken by his voice. Just inside the glass doors, to the left. Get some oxygen in your lungs and hold it. You can do this.

Pulse thundering in his ears, Bill glanced at James,

who had swiveled his wheelchair to face the wall between the kitchen and living room. The old man had his dinky .22 aimed at the cracking paint, ready to back Bill's play. Maybe he wasn't such a bad dude after all.

Bill nodded.

With his free hand, James offered him a middle finger. Like father, like son.

Bill pulled the trigger. What was left of the glass doors spat wood and slapped inward.

James fired his weapon in sync. The .22 made a dull snap, and bits of plaster burst from the kitchen wall. Bill doubted the lead punched through. Even so, Ken would hear two guns and hopefully keep his head down.

Move, move, move.

His feet were already in motion, carrying him through the gunsmoke haze, over bits of paper and glass, the front doorway a bright dream in what suddenly seemed like an impossibly far distance. As he rushed past the doors to the living room, he pivoted and squeezed off four more wild shots, the muzzle-flashes illuminating couches with torn-out stuffing, a broken table, tangled mounds of clothes—but no Ken.

Bill barely had time to consider this mystery before his momentum carried him out the front door and onto the stoop, into cleansing sunlight and New York City air that had never smelled so fine. A savage joy took hold of him, the same kind he imagined Fiona felt at times like this. I'm going to make it out alive, he thought—right before a fist rocketed into his jaw and the world cut to black.

THE PISTOL BARREL was a cold circle against the base of Bill's skull. Face-down in the back of what looked like a very expensive Tesla, Bill felt his stomach clench. His bladder, achingly full, threatened to let go and soak his pants, along with the premium leather seats.

"What did the old man mean about the gold?" Ken asked, grinding the barrel harder into Bill's head.

The funny thing was, Bill felt pretty good about his performance back at the house. Showed a little initiative. Did something in a gunfight other than blunder around like a big idiot. Fiona would have been proud.

With a theatrical sigh, Ken placed his knee onto Bill's lower back and applied every ounce of his two-hundred-plus pounds. Bill pictured his bladder as a water balloon slowly squashed by a rolling tire. "What did he mean?" Ken asked again.

"Is this a rental?" Bill grunted. "Because I'm about to piss myself."

Ken climbed off and yanked Bill out the Tesla's open door in one easy move. They stood in the shadow of a low drawbridge that Bill immediately recognized as the Pulaski, which joined Long Island City with the old Brooklyn neighborhood of Greenpoint. Below the bridge flowed the toxic green waters of the Newtown Creek, which stank like a dead man's fart. Bill scanned the nearby warehouses, the empty parking-lots lined with chain-link fences, and saw nobody. Maybe that was best.

"What are you waiting for?" Barbara asked, leaning against the Tesla's hood.

Wrinkling his nose, Bill unzipped his fly and proceeded to water the pavement between his feet. His bladder deflating felt like pure bliss. "Near Union Square," he said. "But I'm not saying anything more until we make some sort of deal."

Barbara snorted laughter. "Yeah, right."

Bill turned to her, zipping his fly. "Did you kill the old man?"

Barbara wore black leggings and a loose white top, along with her silver watch. "That geezer?" she said. "He opened his window, started firing at me in the yard. Then he shot at Ken. We left. We weren't, like, paid to deal with him, you know?"

"I like how you got slapped back by a guy pushing a hundred," Bill said. "Makes me feel all kinds of warm inside."

Ken shoved the pistol into his waistband and walked over. For the first time Bill noticed the extra padding beneath Ken's right sleeve, where Fiona's bullet had hit him. You're hurt, he thought. Excellent. We can work with that.

His right arm was injured, but Ken's left hand was like a bulldozer claw covered in warm flesh, exerting terrible pressure on the back of Bill's neck. "We like gold. We have stocks to buy, real estate to fund, some furniture we need to have—"

"Dream sofa in linen," Barbara said. "Non-toxic padding. Very important."

"We like gold so much," Ken continued, "that if we get our hands on some, we might even forget about Fiona." He smiled without joy. "What do you say?"

"Cut the shit. I know you're going to kill us."

Ken shrugged. "We just want cold, hard cash, okay? If we make more from gold than your contract, we might overlook the contract."

"You wouldn't. You don't want the Mob on you."

"Think of it this way," Barbara said, her voice sharpening. "You take us where we need to go, you might get a chance to warn Fiona. You die here, you don't get the chance to complicate things."

That makes no sense, Bill thought. No assassin opens up to chance like that. But maybe that's it. Maybe they're too confident. Or totally insane. Either way, what choice do you have?

"A gallery on University," Bill said. "It's in a safe. And I don't have a key."

Barbara and Ken exchanged a whole conversation

in a look. "Get in the front seat," Ken said, shoving Bill toward the car.

Bill did as ordered, while Ken climbed behind the wheel. Barbara slid into the back. Neither bothered to cuff or zip-tie Bill's wrists together.

Ken fastened his seatbelt and tapped the dashboard screen to life with his right hand, wincing slightly as he did so. When a search box appeared, he typed 'Union Square' on the virtual keyboard, and a map popped into view, with a little arrow directing them to the Midtown Tunnel.

"Swanky," Bill said. "How much this cost?"

Ken glanced at Barbara in the rearview mirror. "Borrowed it."

"Okay, but how much does it cost?" When Ken remained stony-faced, Bill smirked and said: "C'mon, man, don't tell me you don't know the prices of things. You're like me: buy the best, cry once." That was flattery; there was nothing unique about the way they dressed. If Bill had to guess, they bought and wore whatever appeared on the covers of the fashion catalogs that hit their doorstep. It was their camouflage.

Ken's stoniness cracked. "Good phrase."

"My Mom taught it to me," Bill said. "And it's true. So come on: how much do you think this car costs? I mean, I'm not an expert, but it looks like it has all the options."

"Low six figures," Ken said, swinging the vehicle in a wide arc. "I want one, but I'm concerned about driving long distances, you know, with a lack of chargers at rest stops. And when you charge up, it takes an hour or something."

"I read they're putting more chargers up."

"Yeah, but that restricts you to certain routes," Barbara piped up. "And we go on little roads a lot, you know. The woods. Part of the job."

"I'm sure," Bill said mildly. The Tesla bumped onto a service road, passing the loading docks of a fortune-cookie factory and a brewery. Ken took a left at the next intersection, onto a broader avenue. No workers, smokers, or joggers on the sidewalk—not that any of them could have helped. Bill knew the exit to the tunnel was coming up, and that a cop car or two usually lurked around there.

As Ken maneuvered the Tesla onto the onramp, he tapped a small lever behind the steering wheel. An upbeat chime sounded, and Ken placed his hands in his lap. "Autopilot," he said. "Welcome to the future."

It took every ounce of Bill's self-control to not squeal as the Tesla merged into a lane. The wheel twisted on its own. Bill gripped his seatbelt, half-expecting the onboard computer to merrily plow them into the car ahead. Instead it braked, matching the speed of traffic heading into the tunnel.

"Let's get some music in here," Ken said, tapping the dashboard. The amplified voice of Chris Martin burst through the speakers, accompanied by a rising organ.

"Please, God, no," Bill said. "Pull my fingernails out, rip out my nuts, but please, no Coldplay."

"Make fun of Coldplay," Barbara said, so close her breath tingled the back of his neck, "and we'll kill you slow."

"Our favorite band," Ken announced, smiling as he cranked the volume.

"I liked them better when they were called U2," Bill said, doing his best to look for cops at the tunnel entrance without moving his head or eyes. He might have been a fugitive from the law, but the prospect of handcuffs and a cell seemed more appealing at the moment than ending up in a ditch with a bullet in his head. "By the way, I have a question."

"Shoot," Barbara said.

"In Havana," he asked. "How'd you find me?"

Barbara laughed. "Those guys you ripped off in the Dominican Republic? Only too happy to give us the laptop they gave you. I know you think you wiped everything on it, but we got enough about your new identities, your cards, everything."

Bill snorted. "Aw, heck."

The tunnel blotted out the sun, a shadow dropping over Ken's face as he smiled. "In Havana, when you tried giving us the slip, we wanted you gone," he said. "Figured out which room you were staying in, put a couple of trackers in your stuff. You were smart enough to dump the clothes, but you weren't going to give up a bag that nice. Trust us, we know."

Barbara touched Bill's ear with a cold finger. "After you left Havana, we called the Dean," she said. "Described the guy you were with. He said it was Don, that he had a father in New York. We took a guess that you'd come here. Risky, but it worked out."

"God, I love this song," Ken said, tapping the music louder and louder. "Third time we saw them in concert, they did this ten-minute version, and it was *amazing*."

"Let me guess," Bill said. "You love Michael Bolton, too? Your playlist have any Kenny G?"

Barbara hit him on the side of the head, softly, and Bill did his best not to flinch. He had spent the trip down the tunnel with his left hand on his right shoulder, thumb hooked into the collar of his shirt, in case she tried to loop that evil bit of wire around his neck. Then again, if he had to spend another thirty minutes listening to this soaring crap, he might ask her to garrote him as a mercy.

A milky glow seeped into the tunnel ahead. The Tesla surfaced into the concrete maze of Midtown. While the autopilot would never beat out a human cab driver for daredevil sangfroid, it managed to avoid other cars as they took a left onto Park Avenue.

Bill gazed out the window at the crowds of pedestrians, the hundreds of harried and tense faces. He envied their everyday problems. "How do you do it?" he asked.

"Do what?" Ken said. Mercy of mercies, he turned the Coldplay down to a murmur.

"Keep your relationship going," Bill said. "You know, with everything."

"You really have to listen," Barbara said. "Oprah always had good advice about that. It's about balance, you know, and giving and receiving. Not just working *hard* on the relationship, but working *smart*."

"Every time we have a teachable moment," Ken said, his eyes finding Barbara in the rearview mirror, "we really sit down and discuss it, you know? And when we're dealing with pressures at work, we make sure to voice those issues, rather than let things build up inside."

"And you have to speak with love in mind," Barbara said. "Are you having communication issues at home?"

"It's been a little tense," Bill admitted.

"Comes down to finding the Zen in the relationship," Ken said. "What the address of this gallery?"

"University and Twelfth." The actual address was two blocks further south.

"Flank." Ken placed his hands on the wheel, and the autopilot chimed. The Tesla whispered to the curb.

"See you in a bit," Barbara said, blowing him an air kiss, and exited onto the street.

As they rejoined the flow of traffic, Ken tapped the autopilot again. The Tesla mingled with a school of yellow taxis swimming downtown. Reaching beneath his shirt, Ken drew his pistol and placed it against his thigh, beneath the level of the window.

Bill's heartbeat accelerated to running pace. "Seems like you two have it together," he said.

Ken shrugged. "All about the listening, man."

A taxi veered into their lane, and the Tesla responded by slamming the brakes. The momentum jolted Ken forward, his grip loose on the pistol.

Bill lashed out with his right fist, aiming for Ken's neck. The assassin might have packed a couple hundred pounds of muscle and bone beneath his tailored suit, but his throat was still a delicate bundle of nerves and vessels.

Bill's knuckles slammed into Ken's windpipe. Ken gagged and dropped the pistol. Bill punched him in the face as hard as he could, slamming Ken's skull against the headrest, before diving for the weapon. His hand brushed the checkered grip when he spied a blur of movement at the edge of his vision—Ken lunging to headbutt him.

With an audible click, Ken's seat-belt locked, pinning his shoulders back, his forehead stopping six inches from Bill's temple.

Bill had a hand flattened on the pistol when Ken stabbed an arm down, slipping a finger onto the trigger. In the tight confines of the car, the gunshot was apocalyptic, world-ending. The bullet plowed into the dashboard to the right of the steering wheel, leaving a smoking hole. Recoil jolted the barrel upwards. Ken's finger twitched again, and a second round vaporized the driver's window in a chunky spray of safety glass.

Even seven-point-five grams of lead traveling faster than the speed of sound through luxury circuits failed to stop Chris Martin serenading their bloody fight. The hot pistol tumbled from their grip, disappearing beneath the pedals. Shifting tactics, Bill drove his shoulder into Ken's torso, hoping to drive the air out of his lungs. It felt like tackling a refrigerator.

Seemingly unfazed by Bill's attempt to play linebacker, Ken wrapped his left hand around Bill's throat. Bill responded by slamming his fists into the bandage on Ken's right arm, hoping to bring the pain.

No luck. Those massive fingers applied industrial pressure directly to Bill's trachea. The world trembled and darkened at the edges. His lungs burning, Bill placed his palms against Ken's chest and pushed as hard as he could. Ken's thumbs eased a bit, affording Bill the faintest sip of oxygen. Then Bill's hands slipped and Ken bulled forward again, to tighten his grip.

Instead of trying to meet Ken on his own terms, Bill planted his right foot against the dashboard and shoved backward with his remaining strength. That worked: he tore free of that iron grip hard enough to slam against his passenger door. Ken's face twisted with rage, his hands slapping the air.

Attack, baby, Fiona urged in his head. Bill took his foot off the dashboard and slammed it into Ken's chest as hard as he could.

In an ordinary fight, a super-killer like Ken would have blocked a move like that easily, and probably snapped Bill's ankle in the bargain. Weakened by pain and that blow to the throat, Ken could only grunt as his body thumped against the driver's door, pinned by Bill's expensive shoe and locked knee.

The Tesla, its robot brain unconcerned by the battle rocking its front seats, continued down Park Avenue at a stately pace. Bill had read enough magazine stories about these cars to know that touching the steering wheel or tapping the pedals would shift the steering back to human control, yet that blue autopilot icon glowed on the dashboard screen. Bill wondered if the first bullet had damaged the electronics.

Ken took a deep breath and tried to shove Bill's leg aside, so Bill rammed his other foot into Ken's chest. Both legs straight, knees locked, Bill braced his shoulders against his door and rose off the seats, seeking maximum leverage. His muscles screamed for mercy.

Ken, failing to budge Bill's locked legs, reached into the footwell. The pistol. If Bill dropped his legs to scramble for it, a freed Ken could do any number of horrible things. If he stayed in place, Ken's long arms would reach the weapon anyway, and then—game over.

No way am I dying to this awful music, Bill thought.

Park Avenue heading south into Union Square had two lanes, plus a far-right one for parking. The Tesla had chosen the middle lane, clear of traffic for the next few blocks. To their left, a pair of white box trucks trundled along, brake lights flaring as they approached the intersection.

Ken's hand rose, the pistol in his grip.

Bill's feet slid a few inches down Ken's sternum. Muscles quaking, Bill extended his legs. Ken had size, but Bill had enough leverage to push the upper half of Ken's body through the shattered driver's window. The rear truck's bumper passed the Tesla. As Chris Martin worked a high note, Ken's head connected with two tons of metal at thirty miles an hour.

That song about peace and harmony climaxed with a meaty crunch.

The pistol clattered out of sight.

Bill drew his aching legs back, relieved when Ken's body remained jammed in place. The prospect of a headless corpse flopping back into the driver's seat, neck painting the cabin with blood, was more than his nerves could take.

The Tesla's sensors, recognizing a red light ahead, braked the car. Bill exhaled loudly and closed his eyes.

Someone screamed, high and shrill.

Bill's eyes snapped open. The windshield framed a family in the crosswalk: a hipster father with a blonde goatee, gripping the handles of a tri-wheeled baby carriage, beside his tattooed wife toting two bags of groceries. The sight of a gore-splattered Tesla seemed to disturb them. The father shrieked again as he pushed the baby carriage for the curb, followed by his gibbering wife.

Stunned by the noise, Bill waved back. Freakout aside, the family did have a point: a car with a headless corpse, idling at one of the city's poshest intersections, was liable to start attracting attention. Especially with cheerful music blaring out its shattered window.

Unbuckling his seat belt, Bill shoved the pistol into his waistband and draped his shirt over the grip. He stepped into the street, closing the Tesla's door behind him. A dozen taxi drivers regarded him with studied coolness. Bill figured a few had come from war-torn countries where the burning of your village is just another Tuesday; on that scale, decapitation via luxury car barely rated a yawn.

The traffic light flicked green, and the Tesla hummed away, bearing headless Ken into the distance. Bill assumed the vehicle would follow whatever route Ken had pre-programmed, and park itself once it reached the final destination. Welcome to the future, filled with dead men at the wheel.

A few pedestrians stopped to snap photos of the passing Tesla with their phones. Ignoring them, Bill adjusted his lapels and walked in the opposite direction.

6

A LONG TIME AGO, Dusty's had dominated a corner a few blocks south of Union Square. Bill remembered it from his early days in the city: a place so old-school it still had an ornate wooden bar, a potbelly stove in one corner, and sooty light-bulbs older than most of the clientele. It attracted a peculiar combination of drinkers: hipster kids on a misguided quest for authenticity, businessmen looking to murder their livers in a hole convenient to their office, and old-timers clinging to a last bit of old New York like shipwrecked sailors clinging to flotsam.

That was all gone now. In its place stood a gleaming cube of steel and smoked glass. The front door, distinguishable from the rest of the translucent front only by the most discrete of handles, had the word 'GALLERY' etched on it, with the open days and hours beneath.

Bill tried the handle. The posted hours said the place was closed, but what if someone was working alone, or expecting a special customer? The door was locked. He ran a thumb over the deadbolt below the handle—possible to pick, if he had the tools. Where was Fiona?

As if summoned, she stepped from between two parked cars and asked: "What happened to you?"

"Ken and Barbara," he said, as she ran a hand down his face, pausing at the scratches on his cheeks.

Fiona glanced around. "Where?"

"Barbara might be close. As for Ken, let's just say he got ahead of himself."

Fiona squinted at him. "What?"

"He tried to be head and shoulders above the rest."

"Start making sense, dear."

"He got his head knocked off by a truck."

Fiona paused. "So he's dead."

"Oh, I hope so."

"You know, you can come out and say it, instead of trying to be James Bond with the puns." She laughed, her palm on his chin. "You're so ridiculous."

"Barbara got out of the car before Ken and I started fighting. She's headed in this direction."

"Then we better move fast," she said, nodding toward a battered white van parked midway down the block. "I got a van."

"How are we getting inside?"

Reaching into her pocket, she said: "Got tools."

"A rock?"

"Ha, you're funny." She drew a small device that looked

like a steel cutout of a pistol, with a long needle for a barrel. Its handle reminded Bill of a miniature caulking-gun.

"Believe it or not," he said, "I've never seen a snap gun before."

"My lockpicking skills have gone to crap," Fiona said, adjusting the brass thumb-wheel on the back of the device. "Not that I was ever great with a rake, anyway." Handing the snap gun to Bill, she dug into her pocket again and extracted a small metal pick, which she slipped into the deadbolt and twisted until the tension felt right.

Fiona returned the snap gun. She slid its tip into the keyway, above the pick, and pulled the trigger—snap, snap, snap. The deadbolt pins popped. She twisted the pick, and the lock popped open.

Gripping the door-handle, Bill asked: "What if there's an alarm?"

"Of course there's an alarm, doofus," Fiona said. "It's already taken care of."

With a final glance at the empty street, Bill pulled the door open. He bowed theatrically, ushering Fiona inside. She smiled and tipped an imaginary hat as she entered the lobby, and Bill's heart leapt. They were getting through this. Everything would be okay.

The lobby was paneled with blonde wood, the reception desk a glass surfboard balanced on a narrow aluminum curve. Bill spied a small white panel embedded in the wall, its lights blinking green, and tensed for a siren.

"Hello?" Fiona called, peeking through the wide doorway that led to the gallery's first room. "I think we're alone."

"How'd you disable it?" Bill asked, locking the door behind them.

"I bet the alarm would be wireless," she said. "It's all the rage these days. No wires, minimal installation, you can even use a remote control to disable it without a code. Simon gave me a gizmo that mimics that remote. I used it before we picked the lock."

"How is Simon these days?"

"Still scary as shit. But he sends his love."

"That's a relief. I'd hate to get on his bad side."

"He's the least of our problems." Fiona ducked into that first room, trailed by Bill. It was the scene of a stop-motion car bombing: chunks of white sedans dangled from the ceiling on nearly invisible wires; blinking fluorescent tubes pierced the wreckage at odd angles, representing physics, pressure, fire. According to the text printed on the wall beside the doorway, the artist, Chun Li, had always been obsessed with the illusion of order in a chaotic world.

They kept walking. At the entrance to the next room hung a small drawing, four inches by five, in a thick white plastic frame. The artist had executed his work with chalk, pencil, and a few ounces of his own blood. The subject was a nude woman on her hands and knees, with what looked like an automobile driveshaft jutting out her mouth.

"Matthew Barney rip-off," Bill said. "But good lines. What do you think, honey?"

Fiona sucked air through her teeth and entered the third room, where black-and-white prints of cow carcasses lined the walls, sharing space with gluey collages of religious icons and porno. In the center of the space, the *pièce de résistance*: an actual human brain in a jar, in a red leather wing chair, facing an old-style television looping a six-second clip of Jerry Seinfeld laughing.

"I hate all of it," Fiona said.

"Hate's a strong word."

"Oh, you like it?"

Bill smiled, showing some teeth. "I'm sure it'd fit right into someone's living room. Like, Hannibal Lecter's."

The fourth room was the largest yet, lit from above by harsh white light. Behind a glass wall to their right, arrow-pierced tigers snarled at them, frozen in the act of leaping, their heavily muscled legs twisted in death. To their left, an unmarked white door: the back office, hopefully. Bill made a beeline for it, while Fiona behind him kept a slower pace, frowning at the dead predators.

As Bill reached for the doorknob, they heard a loud click, followed by a booming voice:

"The lion..."

They spun, startled, ready for the attack.

Behind the tigers, a widescreen flickered with images of the African veldt: lions stalking through the brown grass, sedate rhinos bathing in mud. A nature documentary, another part of the exhibition. The narrator was cultured, British, amused by the hunt.

"...stalks the plains in search of whatever it can find..." Fiona pointed above their heads. "Motion sensor," she said. "It must click on whenever anyone enters the room."

"Any way to shut it off?"

Fiona spread her arms and spun. "You see any buttons around here, hotshot? Maybe behind that door."

Maybe some relationship counseling wouldn't hurt, Bill thought as he opened the white door. In the gloom beyond: wide desks, tall leather chairs, a window that offered a stunning view of a brick wall. The window was open an inch. "We could have just come..."

A fist rocketed out of the darkness, colliding with his nose.

Bill stumbled, face crackling with pain. A pale flash. On instinct his arms rose to protect his face. A glimpse of Barbara, her hand a bright blur. His jaw exploded, and his knees turned to gelatin. He toppled, flashing on the dead cop on the road in Havana. What the hell did she hit me with? What a stupid—

Barbara's shirt exploded and she fell backward.

"Bill?" Fiona called out. The pistol in her hand smoking. Bill was facedown, not bleeding but not moving. She wanted more than anything to kneel and place her hand on his back and feel him breathing, sense the blood thudding through his veins, but the bitch beside him was twitching, still alive, too close at this range for a clean shot with her shaking hands.

Barbara ran her hands over her torn shirt. Mushroomed bits of metal rained to the floor. "Kevlar," she wheezed, tapping the heavy vest beneath the cloth. "Prepared."

"Get up," Fiona said. "Interlace your hands behind your head and move to the left." Not that she had any intention of letting this psycho live. She just wanted a clean shot.

As Barbara followed orders, Bill's hand scratched the polished gallery floor. His fingers skimmed his jaw. The pain was immediate, a gasoline fire beneath his teeth.

Beside his arm, where Barbara dropped it, a compact stun-gun in silver, the kind that fit in the palm of your hand. Nothing like a couple thousand volts to make you feel like crap. "Barb," he rasped.

Barbara met his eyes, her face pinched into a bloodless mask of fury.

"I don't know if you know this," he said. "But Ken really lost his head."

And he grinned.

Barbara kicked him in the face, hard, and Bill flopped backwards.

"That wasn't nice," Fiona said.

"I should have brought my real gun," Barbara said, "and not that little toy. But people can't answer questions when they're dead."

"You're a straight-up psycho, aren't you?" Fiona replied, circling so that Barbara would step away from Bill. Instead the woman held her ground, arms raised away from her body.

"In the car, he said you were having problems," Barbara said. "Do you love him?"

"Talked to a mutual friend," Fiona said, sighting the pistol between her eyes. "Told me you got a boob job with blood money. Doesn't look like it, sweetie. Your chest looks as flat as Ken's pulse-rate."

"I'm going to kill you," Barbara said, and took two steps the left.

Perfect.

Time to end this.

"You'll try, bitch," Fiona said, her finger already tightening on the trigger—but that damn shakiness took hold, her finger loose and weak even as every nerve in her head screamed fire, fire, fire.

Quicker than quick, Barbara darted across the empty space and slammed a fist into Fiona's face. Another into her ribs. Bone cracking in both places. Fiona's hand snapped open, her pistol clattering away, and suddenly she didn't care. The pain deep, blinding—she crumpled to her knees, choking for air—

Barbara tried driving a knee into Fiona's nose. Fiona raised a hand to block it, the impact shaking her arm. With her other hand, she popped the blade from her belt buckle. Barbara spied the steel a microsecond before Fiona swung, leapt back.

Standing on the balls of her feet, Fiona slipped the weapon between the second and third knuckles of her right hand. Forced herself to take a deep breath with burning lungs, to tighten the quaking muscles in her arms. *Please don't shake*, she tried to tell her body. *Please, we need to live.*

"You arrogant fuck," Barbara eyed the pistol on the floor. "You're not half as good as they said you were."

With her free hand, Fiona made a come-hither gesture. "Come on."

If Barbara leapt for the pistol, she would turn her back on Fiona. They both knew it. Barbara tore off her shirt, revealing her pockmarked black vest and a T-shirt beneath; she wrapped the shredded cloth loosely around her right forearm, to blunt Fiona's blade.

"You're boring me," Fiona said.

Barbara charged, and Fiona raised her knife, expecting the trick, the feint. Barbara shoved her wrapped forearm in Fiona's face, hiding her movement as her other hand went for the knife. After she grabbed the wrist of Fiona's knife-hand, Barbara would shove a knee into Fiona's stomach. Fiona would have done exactly the same thing.

Instead of slashing blindly, Fiona sidestepped and grabbed Barbara's wrist, and pushed. Barbara slammed face-first into the wall. Fiona dropped her knife, gripped all that shiny hair, and smashed Barbara's head into the floor, into the wall, smashed until everything was a red mess, smashed until her forearms were covered with tabs of skin and white bits of bone.

Afterwards Fiona lay there for a minute, struggling for breath as her adrenaline turned weak and sour. Her nose throbbed, warm wetness trickling out. That's what you get for your stupid hands shaking. Talk all you want about being a badass: in the end you're just another fuck-up. *Oh, is Fiona's poor little nose bleeding?* Good. Let it bleed. You earned that. You earned everything you got.

On the far wall of the gallery, the documentary about Africa kicked back to life, the sonorous tones of the narrator rumbling over Fiona's gasping form. "In the wilderness," he informed the room, "the battle for survival is often quick and merciless, and the only reward is the victor gets to fight another day…"

"No shit, buddy," Fiona called out. "Tell me something I don't know."

Spitting a mouthful of blood, she rose to her knees.

"The hyena," the narrator continued, "is a master at this sort of survival."

Slapping a red hand against the wall, Fiona struggled to her feet, her chest burning. There was always the danger that a broken rib could slice through an organ, or peel open an artery. She would have to risk it: she had promises to keep, and miles to go before she could head to the emergency room.

"I am a master at survival," she hissed through gritted teeth, driving her foot into Barbara's belly for old times' sake. The body skidded a few inches, barely worth the bolt of pain that shot up Fiona's spine.

"The hyena will use whatever cover it can take to approach its prey," the narrator boomed.

"Smart animal," Fiona said, and began the long odyssey over to Bill. It felt as if someone had filled her stomach with gasoline and struck a match, but her legs and arms still worked just fine, thank you very much. She knelt and touched Bill's neck, and his eyes fluttered open.

"Barbara," he murmured.

"Splattered."

"That's what they get for Coldplay."

"Don't get you, hon." Patting him on the top of the head, Fiona stood and hobbled for the office, leaving Bill to roll onto his stomach and shove himself upright.

With the lights on, the office was a standard-issue space, startling only in its blandness after the weird sights in the gallery. The furniture and light fixtures were gleaming plastic and chrome, but the brick walls and gray floorboards seemed untouched from the bar days. As she paced the floor, Fiona saw some of Barbara's blood drying on her shirt. She felt no guilt. Barbara had once been meat that could think. Now she was just meat. Meanwhile Fiona had to find this loot and get out of here.

When she believed she had the right spot, she took

a deep breath and held it, willing as much of the pain away as possible. She slipped her knife between the floorboards and levered until one popped loose with a loud crack and faint puff of dust. Bill knelt beside her to yank the adjacent ones loose. They found dirty insulation, tangles of dust and litter, the translucent curves of mouse bones. Bill swept those away to expose the rusty angle of the safe.

The front of the safe featured gold trim and the word 'NICHOLL' in fine script, along with a keyhole. Massive hinges held the double doors in place. Bill brushed the dirt away from the lock.

"Here's the key," Fiona said, handing it over.

Bill tried to slip the key into the slot. "It doesn't fit." He glanced at her, eyebrow raised, and she made a show of raising a hand to slap him. Even that gesture sent a sharp bolt of pain up her arm.

"Think the old man was trying to screw us?" Bill asked.

Fiona shook her head. "Nah. He probably just forgot which key. Hold on, Simon gave me something for this, but it's in the van." Fiona stood and hobbled out of the room. Bill heard the front door of the gallery open, close, open again. She reappeared with a shrink-wrapped block of gray putty. A stamped label on the front said 'SEMTEX.' Taped to it, a bundle of black and red wires.

Bill took the bundle of plastic explosive from her, turning it in his hands. "You scamp, this is cheating."

"Lighten up," Fiona said, bending to brush more dust from the hinges. "It'll be fun."

7

BACK AT THE HOUSE, James clapped his wrinkled hands and laughed at the sight of the bag plopped in the kitchen doorway. The cops had left long ago, but a few strands of police tape still fluttered loosely in the front hallway. Raindrops spattered the dusty kitchen window. All you need is a hundred-year flood, Bill thought, and that glass might actually get clean.

Fiona knelt and unzipped the bag. "Heavy as hell," she said. "Good thing we had a vehicle."

"Got no idea what I'm going to do with it," James said. "But probably safer in my yard than underneath some pansy's gallery, am I right?"

"Yeah, galleries are dangerous," Fiona said. Cupping a gnarled lump of gold in her hands, she limped over to the kitchen table. Don shoved a stack of stained takeout menus aside so she could place the treasure in front of James, whose purple lips split into a wide yellow grin.

"You know, when we went in and shot all those Nazi bastards, we weren't looking to get rich," James said. "But considering how much killing we had to do, I figure nobody would begrudge us taking a little something-something."

"No doubt," Bill said, turning to Fiona. "So what now?"

"We take our share," Fiona said, nodding to the bag on the floor, "and leave. You cool with that? You better be, because that's the deal."

"Maybe with all that money," Don said, "you can hire a nurse or something."

James froze. His grin faded. "Excuse me, boy?"

"I have to go back south." Don shoved his chair back. "We got a factory to run, remember? And now we have a real shot at being profitable again, thanks to my cut of this."

"You're leaving me?" James's lips quavered. His hand retreated beneath his blanket.

"Sorry," Don said, not sounding sorry at all.

The rain drummed hard on the window, churning the dirt into brown streaks. The yard beyond dissolved to gray. Bill was suddenly aware of how every heartbeat made his sore muscles ache and twinge. We need to get out of here, he thought. A half-hour to the airport, and a couple of hours to someplace new. We can take another chance at living, instead of just existing.

"When your grandfather was sick, I took care of him every day," James said. "I went through some miserable shit, because I believed in duty." He jabbed a gnarled finger at Bill and Fiona. "These two, they came back with my gold. Didn't have to, but they did. You could learn something from them."

"Not so sure about that," Bill said, and Fiona elbowed him in the ribs.

"If you didn't want to be alone in your old age, maybe you shouldn't have been such a hardass," Don said. "I want my cut. I have a plane to catch."

A silver flash as James's arm swooped in a tight arc that ended with Don's hand, outstretched on the table. A long blade buried between Don's second and third knuckles, Don screaming shrill as a fire alarm as James roared with youthful vigor: *"There's your cut, you little shit!"*

ACKNOWLEDGMENTS

NO WRITER IS AN ISLAND (no matter how much they might believe otherwise). In writing Slaughterhouse Blues, I relied on feedback from Jen Conley and Angel Luis Colón, who offered excellent advice (even if it meant rewriting the last third of the book). I'm also indebted to Ron Earl Phillips, publisher and editor extraordinaire, for placing his faith in this multi-part odyssey of two crazy criminals.

While many of the locations in this book, such as Estelí, are real, I took some liberties with geography in the name of pacing and plot. For any egregious inaccuracies, dear reader, blame me. And if you get the chance, visit Havana; it's an incredible city, pulsing with life.

This book was written to the tunes of the *Buena Vista Social Club* and *Nick Cave & The Bad Seeds*.

NICK KOLAKOWSKI IS the Derringer- and Anthony-nominated author of Maxine Unleashes Doomsday and Boise Longpig Hunting Club, as well as the Love & Bullets trilogy of novellas. He lives and writes in New York City. Visit him virtually at nickkolakowski.com.

SHOTGUN HONEY
FICTION WITH A KICK